FROM NIGHT TO KNIGHT

ONE MAN'S JOURNEY from the dark night of materialism and spiritual uncertainty to the bounty of becoming a Knight of Bahá'u'lláh, to further trials and tribulations in a life devoted to mass teaching – this is Jenabe Esslemont Caldwell's story. Whether pioneering in the frozen wastes of the Aleutian Islands, in the heat of Mexico or elsewhere in the spiritual desert of mid-twentieth-century materialism, Caldwell shares with the reader not only the tests, but also the indescribable gifts of a life dedicated to the service of the Bahá'í Faith. A book about trust and growth, about good judgement and misunderstanding, it is a highly personal and moving account of 'Caldwell's Progress.'

ABOUT THE AUTHOR: Jenabe Caldwell was born in the state of Montana and has lived in Alaska, Mexico and Japan as well as the United States. His pioneering and mass teaching have taken him to fifty-four countries over the past forty years. Jenabe Caldwell has five children and now lives in Japan.

In memory of the illustrious

Áqá Buzurg-i-Níshápúrí of Khurásán,

known as Badí', named a Knight by the

Pen of Bahá'u'lláh and a shining example for all

the Knights who follow in his footsteps.

FROM NIGHT TO KNIGHT

Jenabe E. CALDWELL

ONEWORLD

OXFORD

From Night To Knight

Oneworld Publications Ltd
(Sales and Editorial)
185 Banbury Road
Oxford OX2 7AR
England

Oneworld Publications Ltd
(U.S. Sales Office)
County Route 9, P.O. Box 357
Chatham, N.Y. 12037, U.S.A.

ISBN 1-85168-048-9

Cover illustration and book design by Michael Sours
Printed and bound in Great Britain
by Guernsey Press

FOREWORD

THROUGHOUT THE BAHÁ'Í WORLD in 1953, hearts throbbed with longing and minds quickened with dreams of destinations and destinies in response to the beloved Guardian's call for pioneers to open territories virgin to the Bahá'í Faith. The spiritual reward, to be accompanied by the correlative title of 'Knight of Bahá'u'lláh,' would be great.

The Guardian's cablegram of 28 May 1953, addressed to the Bahá'í World, contained these thrilling words:

> The dispersal, immediate, determined, sustained and universal, throughout the unopened territories of the planet, is the paramount issue challenging the spirit and resources of the privileged prosecutors of the Ten Year Plan in the course of the current year . . . Once again I appeal to members of all communities to arise and enlist, ere the present opportunity is irretrievably lost, in the army of Bahá'u'lláh's crusaders. The hour is ripe to disencumber themselves of worldly vanities, to mount the steed of steadfastness, unfurl the banner of

*renunciation, don the armor of utter consecration to
God's Cause, gird themselves with the girdle of a chaste
and holy life, unsheathe the sword of Bahá'u'lláh's
utterance, buckle on the shield of His love, carry as sole
provision implicit trust in His promise, flee their
homelands, and scatter far and wide to capture the
unsurrendered territories of the entire planet . . .*

This cablegram also set forth the special accolade to be
awarded to such intrepid souls:

*Planning to inscribe in chronological order, the names
of the spiritual conquerors on an illuminated Roll of
Honor, to be deposited at the entrance door of the inner
Sanctuary of the Tomb of Bahá'u'lláh, as a permanent
memorial of the contribution by the champions of His
Faith . . . Anticipate making periodic announcements of
the names of the valiant knights upon their arrival at their
posts to discharge their historic missions . . . SHOGHI.*

A few months prior to this cabled announcement and
to the formal presentation of the Ten Year Crusade to
the Bahá'í world, I made my initial teaching trip outside
my home state of California into the South. There I
met a young couple with two small boys, very obvious-
ly soon to be blessed with another child. Although the
exact goals of the Crusade were not yet announced,
Bahá'ís generally knew that worldwide teaching goals
would be presented at the coming International
Conferences scheduled for the Ridván period and that
they would be called upon to fulfill them.

The young husband was completing a special electronics course and spoke enthusiastically of his

intention to take his family to some distant post armed with his new profession. Clearly what he was primarily armed with was a fiery desire to share the teachings of Bahá'u'lláh with the whole world. His young wife, although quiet and contained, exuded a dedication and a purpose equally staunch. It was a long time ago and I no longer remember their exact words, but I well remember the strength of their spirit and intentions.

It was therefore with a sense of inevitability that at the following International Conference held in Chicago, I heard the young father of the family shout from the conference platform that he and his wife and their two and eight-ninths children offered themselves as pioneers.

This couple was Jenabe and Elaine Caldwell. The two children on hand were Daniel and David Caldwell. The child offered as a pioneer even before his outward appearance on this earth was Mark Caldwell, currently a dedicated Bahá'í teacher who pilots an airplane into the remote villages of Alaska to bring them the teachings of Bahá'u'lláh. The first two boys, as well as two daughters born much later, have also followed this same path of dedication.

Shortly after this conference, I heard that the Caldwell family, which had hoped to pioneer to the warm South Pacific (their home state was Montana, and it gets pretty cold up there) had instead journeyed to the Aleutian Islands of Alaska! It seemed that Hand of the Cause Dorothy Baker, faced with the difficulty of procuring volunteers for those harsh and forbidding islands, had telephoned Jenabe and Elaine as representative of the National Spiritual Assembly of the United States, asking if they could accept this challenge. They did accept. Someone, knowing of my interest in the Caldwells, sent me a color slide of the family as they set forth from Anchorage, Alaska to their Aleutian post in Unalaska. The group photo was very touching – the two solemn little boys, Mama and Papa, the latter with a two-week-old baby boy in his arms. Even though Mama and Papa had determined smiles on their faces, all looked a little tired and very vulnerable.

It was four years later, in another Ridván period, that I had the privilege of being on pilgrimage at the Bahá'í World Center in Haifa. For seven of the nine nights of my pilgrimage I was a guest at the dinner table of Shoghi Effendi, and for the last few of those nights, I chanced to be the only pilgrim present. Among the indelible memories of this memorable time was this. Before I left, the Guardian asked that the Roll of Honor of the Knights of Bahá'u'lláh, that list of the courageous souls who had already responded to his call, be brought to the table.

When the Roll came Shoghi Effendi opened it full length on the long dining table. "Look, Mrs. Mayberry," he said. "And when you return to the United States, tell the Bahá'ís that a few places on the Roll are still vacant where their names may yet be added. When the Roll is complete it will be placed for all time at the threshold of Bahá'u'lláh's Shrine."

I looked, transfixed not only by the wonder of actually seeing the scroll but by the wonder of seeing the Guardian himself gaze upon it with such pride – a pride that seemed to me to be infused with the heady elixir of triumph.

And there, on that marvelous scroll, shimmering through the mist of my unshed tears, were the names of that gallant young couple, Jenabe and Elaine Caldwell.

This may give you a faint intimation of what Jenabe means by traversing the 'night' of man-oriented living into the God-oriented adventure of becoming one of those 'Knights' so highly praised and lovingly encouraged by the Guardian of our Faith.

Florence V. Mayberry
Oxnard
California

PREFACE

*I bear witness, O my God, that Thou hast created me
to know Thee and to worship Thee. I testify at this moment,
to my powerlessness and to Thy might, to my poverty and to
Thy wealth.
There is none other God but Thee, the Help in Peril,
the Self-Subsisting.*

Bahá'u'lláh

On every side the darkness of negativity has enveloped mankind. This darkness is blacker than the voids of space. Catch phrases such as 'God is dead', 'religion is an empty word', 'God is a crutch for the weak and fearful', 'religion is the opiate of the people', are current favorites of our generation. The veils of night have so enveloped humanity that outwardly, not a glimmer of light can be seen. Yet, in reality, behind the veils of this darksome night, stands revealed the very manifestation of light – Bahá'u'lláh – shining with a brilliant radiance unequaled by countless suns. This light holds within itself the power to completely dissolve, dissipate and shatter forever the veils surrounding us. The bats of darkness will flee in consternation and be consumed by the radiance of God's revelation.

My lack of literary ability will soon be made abundantly clear, but love – deep, tender, spiritual love for each and every one of you, love that is beyond time and place – compels me to take up the pen and share with you one soul's struggle from darkness to light. From reading this account, I hope you may find the strength and hope to persevere in your quest. My prayer is that each of you will be able to pierce the veils of self and material desires and, on the celestial wings of certitude, gain admittance into the Kingdom of Light. I can only wish that my soul be a ransom for what the Blessed Beauty was made to endure, and my life be a sacrifice for all your peace and happiness.

Jenabe E. Caldwell
Utsunomiya City, Japan
October 1992

PROLOGUE

EVALENA'S STORY

M Y MOTHER, Evalena Beaver Caldwell, was born in a sod house in Sioux Indian country, Aurora County, South Dakota. She only went as far as the third grade in school. What follows is her own story of how she came to know of the Bahá'í Faith.

On a particular evening, with my three baby girls asleep, I was day-dreaming over the dishes when I was startled by a knock at the door. Into the kitchen came my very excited neighbor, clutching the evening paper.

"Oh, Evalena!" she cried. "You must come with me this evening!" She opened the paper and read, "New divine revelation, meeting in the Placer Hotel, 8 p.m., admission free."

Oh, for heaven's sake! What next? I thought to myself, but replied, "I really can't. The girls are asleep and I don't have a baby-sitter."

"That's all right," she answered. "My eldest girl will look after them."

"Well, you know I'm a Catholic and it's against my religion to go to this kind of meeting without permission from the priest."

"Oh, come on," she insisted. "Just because someone is teaching about God doesn't mean you can't listen. And besides, Matt won't be home from work until midnight and it might be exciting. Please say you'll come!"

So, in spite of myself and only to please my persistent neighbor, I decided to humor her. Even now, how can I sufficiently thank God for His guidance? I stand thunderstruck to contemplate what my life would have been had I not gone. How often does one's life stand at such a crossroads? Only my concern for my neighbor's happiness brought me to the ocean of life.

The meeting was held in one of those anonymous hotel rooms, dingy in the extreme. As I found out later, the Bahá'í speaker was visiting all the capital cities in the United States, under the direction of Shoghi Effendi. Praise be to God that at this moment of my life I was in Helena, Montana. My friend and I were the only two in attendance. At the door, we almost turned back.

How can I ever describe that meeting! The woman speaker at first appeared very nondescript, but received us with a love and tenderness I had not experienced before. When she began to speak, that hotel room surpassed royal palaces and her voice was that of a pure angel. My soul was set afire that night . . . Time stopped for me and, like a person who had been left aimless and adrift in the desert, I began to drink from the heavenly spring of the true water of life. What vistas of light she opened before my eyes! When it was time to go, she gave us each a kiss, assured us of her prayers and gave both of us cards listing the ten principles of the Bahá'í Faith.

Now our roles were reversed – I was so excited I wanted to shout to the world these new glad tidings, while my friend, nonplussed at my response, said, "What a quaint little old lady!" Strangeness upon strangeness. Surely the words, "He guideth whomsoever He willeth" had never been more true.

I waited up that night for Matt. I had never known such happiness as filled my heart. I am sure that when my husband finally did come home, he must have thought I had lost my mind, for at first all I could say was, "You should have seen her; you should have heard her!"

Finally, I was able to explain that a new Messenger of God had appeared on the earth and these were His teachings. I then handed Matt the little card of ten principles. What keen spiritual insight my husband had! Upon reading those principles, his first words were, "It is about time." Then both he and I, drawing only upon the fleeting words of that angel of light, sat down together and penned our dedication of faith, requesting more teachings of Bahá'u'lláh, our newly found Beloved.

Praise and glory be to God, who hears the prayers of the least of His servants and is prone to answer! On the seventh of Kalimát, 82 Bahá'í Era (7 August 1926), God fulfilled the innermost yearning of our hearts and sent us our longed-for baby boy. Matt and I had deepened in our beloved faith, and our greatest wish and highest aspiration was that this new-born gift of God would one day arise and champion the Cause of

Bahá'u'lláh. At that time, we also had the added bounty of having as a visitor in the United States that great but humble Persian teacher, Jinábi Fádil-i-Mazandarání. My husband begged Mr. Fádil to bestow his name upon our new son. With complete and pure humility, Jinábi Fádil was disinclined to do this. As the day for the naming ceremony drew near, my persistent husband continually pestered his guest, reminding him that the Americans were destined to become the spiritual descendants of the Dawnbreakers . . . and wasn't this same Jinábi Fádil one whose lameness was attributed to the bastinado, so cruelly administered as to permanently cripple both feet? Wasn't he considered one of the greatest western teachers by both 'Abdu'l-Bahá and Shoghi Effendi? What great bounty, Matt reasoned, to have a son follow in the footsteps of so great a blessed one. Finally, this pure soul asked my husband if he would be content to name his son Jenabe Esslemont. Matt and I were both overjoyed with this selection, and being ignorant of the Persian language, did not realize that this humble teacher had merely called the child 'His Eminence Esslemont'. Only that pure soul and God know the prayers he uttered as he held our tiny newborn babe in his hands.

When I shared my mother's story with Hand of the Cause Amatu'l-Bahá Rúhíyyih Khánum, she thought that the woman who gave my mother the Bahá'í message could have been Martha Root. In 1923 Martha Root went across America by train and stopped at all the capital cities en route. Helena is the capital of Montana. Mother did not remember the lady's name, but the time was right.

Both my mother and father, until the end of their earthly lives, remained staunch and fervent supporters of the Cause of Bahá'u'lláh, being the first Bahá'í couple enrolled in the state of Montana.

The account is fragmentary and I cannot vouch for its complete accuracy as Mother has passed on and cannot verify it all. From Hand of the Cause Mr. Khadem I learned that my namesake Jináb-i Fáḍil had no family that accepted the Cause he championed so vigorously. I pray God that one day both he and Dr. Esslemont, in the realm of glory, will be able to accept me with pride as their true son. Please God, that I can be worthy.

CHAPTER

1

MY VERY FIRST MEMORY of this life took place when I was two or three years old. My father was not home and mother was alone in their bed, the soft light of dawn slowly filling the room. I carefully climbed over the railing of my crib, toddled to the old apple box that mother used for a night stand, found her prayer book and glanced up to see her watching me. She threw back the covers and lifted me into her arms, took the prayer book and began to read to me. Some of the prayers I would try to repeat. The love and warmth of Mother, the security, the peace that pervaded my tiny heart as the early morning sun crept into the room, will never be forgotten. Mother, having little education, was not a good reader but she was simple and pure. Her love and sincerity gave meaning to words that neither she nor I understood. Suddenly the room seemed full of an unearthly light and my tiny body tingled all over. This was my first experience of a world that surpassed ours – so complete, so pure, so near unto God. That morning I was transported into a heavenly realm. It impressed me so profoundly that I will carry the blessed memory through all eternity. Every detail of that room is still as clear and fresh in my mind as on the day it happened.

As I grew older, the most precious time of all was during Sunday School. Not only did my father conduct the Sunday School class himself, but he was guided by that selfless soul Victoria Bedkin, known among the Bahá'í children as Auntie Victoria. How richly she endowed the Bahá'í children of the United States! The ink drawings she made so freely were to me the most desirable possessions. When one of us had memorized the verse on a drawing, we could keep it, and I was able to fill an entire box with her lovely work. Before the time of the committees, she carried the Herculean task of child education, all alone, and mainly at her own expense. She served our Beloved Cause to the best of her ability. I shall always be indebted, along with many others, to Victoria for the bounty of her love, beauty and devotion.

There is a story about Auntie Victoria that circulated through the American Bahá'í community shortly before she passed on to the Abhá Kingdom. It appears that in our baby days of forming assemblies, and the birth pangs of the administration, the National Spiritual Assembly decided to form a Children's Education Committee and did not appoint Auntie Victoria to it. Notwithstanding, that staunch warrior kept her love and nourishment flowing to the children who had grown to love her. Finally, in exasperation (so the story goes), the National Spiritual Assembly wrote to Shoghi Effendi advising him that Auntie would not quit teaching the children. Shoghi Effendi, ever with his finger on the pulse, replied that they must leave her alone. All I can add is this: my life is much richer because of her.

Then came the great depression. Many were the nights our family went to bed hungry – no work, no income. We only had the wealth of the knowledge of God to sustain us. During these hard and trying times a stalwart pioneer, Fred Mortenson, would come to visit – often arriving after riding in a box car, carrying a well-worn carpet bag. He would spend a few days with us and then move on to Spokane, Seattle or Portland. When he came, it was always like a breath of springtime. He had the bounty of knowing 'Abdu'l-Bahá, and he and my parents would sit up late into the night talking of the Cause they loved so much. I am sure it was these selfless visits that went a long way, not only to deepen and strengthen my parents, but also to give them the courage to endure the hard times of that era.

In desperation, my parents sent me away, at the age of only nine, to work in a dairy, and so I entered what could at best be called twentieth-century slavery. I worked twelve to sixteen hours per day, but the job supplied milk for my parents and sisters. This time became the beginning of a long, black night for me. I was cut off from the spiritual sustenance of my home and family and set adrift in the world of materialism. From the dairy, I shuttled from job to job, unable to continue my education, until finally the horror of horrors came when I was swept into the vortex of the Second World War.

I am sure that the past hundred years in the history of humanity will, in the future, be branded as the most barbaric and savage ever. We contemplate the so-called tribal societies and religions in which a young man or maiden in the prime of life was sacrificed to a fertility god by having his or her heart cut out. We cry in righteous indignation: Oh, how savage! What cruel barbarians! Then we send 100,000 young people in the prime of life to be sacrificed at the altar of nationalism. Or we drop a nuclear bomb on a town, sacrificing millions. Oh God, have mercy upon us. Reason has fled and owls of night feed on the carrion of the souls of men. Is the false god of the tribal religions any more false than the modern idols we worship? I experienced firsthand the heart-rending brutality of man's inhumanity to man and, although sunk into the very blackest of nights, found my early childhood training gave me an infinitesimal glimmer of the oneness of mankind, and thus sustained me through this period.

As I was living away from home, I did not declare my belief in Bahá'u'lláh at the age of fifteen as is customary in many Bahá'í homes. The yearnings of my heart for those early awakenings of spiritual truth and nearness to God had kept me going from church to church, but they did not give my soul the nourishment it so longed for. Because of the bitterness and hate I had experienced, I was determined either to find a real and valid reason for life, or terminate my own life with my own hand. I felt that if what I had endured was a criterion for life, then life itself was a sham and an empty letter.

I had left home a boy, and returned a grown man only to find my father on his death bed. As sick as he was, none of his ardor or enthusiasm for the Cause of God had waned. Somehow or other, as I shared my heartache and disillusionment with my parents, with their characteristic love and warmth, they drew me back from the horror and ahead toward that nearness to God I so desperately needed. As my father spoke, I was able, momentarily, to part the veil of my dark night and briefly glimpse reality and light.

As I left home for the last time, I said to my father, "Oh, how I wish I could believe you! It's so beautiful, but if it were true surely all of mankind, with all the problems there are in the world, would hasten to partake of God's life-giving medicine." I feared he had been blinded by his love for Bahá'u'lláh and I was firmly convinced that mankind would not, knowingly or otherwise, forfeit such a God-given bounty, as its sickness was fast approaching the state of hopelessness. I assured my father that I would search the teachings, without being blinded by such love as he was, and I would then show him the error of his ways. The last words my father ever spoke to me were these: "I am not worried about you, my son, for surely God will lead you home."

How blind and arrogant I was! I thought that I, a mere speck of dust, would succeed where others more learned than myself had failed! I could have brought such joy to my father had I, with the insight he possessed, arisen and embraced the Cause of the Almighty as spontaneously as he and mother did. Alas, this was not to be. I took some Bahá'í literature and first read it with a critical and jaundiced eye. Then, as I began reading the writings of Bahá'u'lláh and 'Abdu'l-Bahá, I was like a thirsty man coming to the sea of life, and, although my soul was fired with the teachings of God for this day, I nevertheless was too enmeshed in the black night to realize it.

At this point, I believe it is necessary to mention the Bahá'í principle of the individual investigation of truth. This principle of Bahá'u'lláh is to last man a full thousand years or more, and from my own experience, I must state that it is even more important for future Bahá'í children than for non-Bahá'ís. Each individual must seek and come to the fountain of life through his own efforts. When we are born into the rare atmosphere of a Bahá'í home, it is all too easy for a child to accept the Cause, based on the love and happiness generated by the believers. Thus, he becomes a 'Sunday Bahá'í' without that deep, spiritual reality that can change religion into a daily way of life. Already in less than 150 years this principle has been overlooked in many Persian, and none too few American Bahá'í homes. Children are taught the laws and truth of Bahá'u'lláh's message, but this universal law of individual investigation of the truth has been clearly neglected. I pray that all Bahá'í families will steadily add this critical teaching, with all of its subtle implications.

Alas for me, I did not immediately follow my newly found beloved after my own independent investigation, but again went off chasing those chimera: the god of education, god of matrimony, and god of worldly success and achievement. Upon attaining each goal I found but a shell, and the reality seemed to elude me. I was now a father myself, wanting my children to have the same type of spiritual life that I had experienced. The next time I came upon the ocean of life, both my wife and I jumped in. After much study and investigation, we accepted the Cause of Bahá'u'lláh completely and without reservation. The occasion of the piercing of the veils, and our birth as believers, took place in the year 106 of the Bahá'í Era (1950) in the state of Washington.

CHAPTER

2

MY WIFE, ELAINE, AND I, with our first son, were the first Bahá'í pioneers to live in Eugene, Oregon, and began, to the best of our ability, to serve the Cause of God. We later moved to Great Falls, Montana, which was a goal of the Guardian's second Seven Year Plan, where we were able to help save the Local Spiritual Assembly. Here we deepened our experience in the administration, and our second son was born.

At this time, I had one unnerving experience. Our Regional Teaching Committee decided to open up a new city and I volunteered to be the speaker, as I had three or four days off from my work at a time. One of the Bahá'ís made arrangements in Deerlodge, Montana and I was to make a circuit from Great Falls through to Butte, speaking at cities along the route. There were no believers in Deerlodge, but arrangements had been made for me to speak in the home of a woman who had no previous knowledge of the Faith. The meeting had been advertised in the local paper. As so often happens, no one else came and this young woman was my sole

audience. Since she was unfamiliar with the Faith, I
gave her the message. This was my first experience
with a truly receptive soul. How her eyes shone with
wonder, and what a happy and joyful time we had! I
will never forget how eager she was for literature, and
as I left to go on to Butte she stood by the table with a
truly angelic appearance.

Word preceded me to Butte of her sudden death.
Within five minutes of my departure, a blood clot
reached her brain, killing her instantaneously. This was
but the first of many and various experiences where I
have been urged and guided to fulfill a particular task
that must be done within a certain time. Praise be to
God that I had been there to proffer the everlasting
cup to this ready and expectant soul.

However, all our teaching was not victory. Our
local Spiritual Assembly slowly disintegrated because
of believers moving away and there was no new
interest or even contacts. Firesides bloomed, then died;
public meetings were washouts. We had united prayer
efforts and individual prayer efforts, to no apparent
avail.

That year, during our vacation, my wife and I
attended the Bahá'í Summer School session at
Geyserville in California. This was our first taste of the
complete Bahá'í life. Surely we entered the gates of
heaven, where on all sides rang peace, peace, peace.
One day I was sitting out under the big tree with that
true handmaiden of the Cause of God, Valeria Nichols.
She served the Faith in the second Seven Year Plan, the
Ten Year Crusade and has been valiantly pioneering
since the Nine Year Plan. Valeria was telling me the
story of how she had answered the call of our Guardian

during the second Seven Year Plan. She described all of her frustrations with visas and authorities and how she finally secured a visa for a very short visit to Portugal. The visa was extended, and later when she finally had to leave, she left behind a Local Spiritual Assembly in Lisbon. I thought that if this could be done in far-off Portugal, it could be repeated in Great Falls. I said, "Val, you must have a secret. Whatever you did I want to know about!"

Her plain and simple answer has become one of the strongest guiding principles of my life. She replied, "Jenabe, I didn't do anything. I was helpless. First, I put all my trust and faith in the Hands of Bahá'u'lláh, for where else could I turn? To strengthen this trust, I arose every morning at dawn, walked the streets and said the 'Tablet of Ahmad' nine times."

I had read and reread many times the words of Bahá'u'lláh in regard to putting all your trust and confidence in God as the best of helpers, and it always seemed to me some far-off goal, unattainable and distant. Now I sat with my true Bahá'í sister, who told me she did it, as if it was the most natural thing in the world — which, of course, it is. As I thought and meditated about our problems in Great Falls, it became quite apparent that we poor, weak creatures were trying to do it ourselves; even our prayers had been that *we* might achieve our goals for the Cause of God. Armed with this new perspective, my wife and I returned refreshed, each with added understanding of the truth that *God doeth whatsoever He willeth I lay all my affairs in Thy hand.*

My wife and I subsequently arose every morning at dawn, which in itself was an enriching experience and, alternating, we would say that powerful 'Tablet of Ahmad' nine times. Sometimes I would leave my wife with the children, and I would drive out through the streets of Great Falls saying the Tablet; on these days we jointly said it eighteen times. Within a few days after the completion of our nineteen-day prayer effort came a wire from our National Spiritual Assembly stating that, being aware of our critical situation in maintaining our Assembly, they were sending us help in the person of Kathryn Frankland.

CHAPTER
3

KATHRYN HAD KNOWN 'Abdu'l-Bahá and had even ridden on the train from San Francisco to Oakland with Him, her baby sitting on His lap. She had also gone on pilgrimage in the time of 'Abdu'l-Bahá. Needless to say, Kathryn's soul was fired with her love for the Master and the Cause of God.

She arrived in Great Falls during a cold spell. Kathryn was a tiny little thing, her body deteriorated with age, so that all that was left was a stack of very brittle bones covered with skin and all held together with a brace. She jokingly called this brace her 'harness'. When I met her at the train, I warned her: "Kathryn, although the weather is cold, nothing is as cold as the hearts of the people of Great Falls."

Her eyes were a bright and brilliant blue and these eyes shot fire. She said, "Don't you worry. Bahá'u'lláh guides me, Bahá'u'lláh guides me."

She also had two of the heaviest suitcases I was ever obliged to carry. Subsequently, when she was settled in her hotel room, consisting of bed, dresser, moth-eaten chair and lavatory (the bathroom was at the end of the hall, shared by all tenants), I was privileged to watch her unpack. First, out came books. There was not just one copy but several of each, such as *Gleanings from the Writings of Bahá'u'lláh* and *Bahá'u'lláh and the New Era*. Then, wrapped within her clothes, was the finest and daintiest set of china I had ever seen — consisting of teapot, cups, saucers and tiny plates. Next to appear was a hot plate and tea kettle, then pictures of her loved ones, including four or five of 'Abdu'l-Bahá and the Greatest Name, and of course, clothes. In half an hour that room, with its books, pictures, and so on looked as though it had been lived in for many years. Just the way she looked at 'Abdu'l-Bahá's picture was a joy to see. Such love and tenderness shone in her face and eyes. How she loved the Master! When I discovered that she knew 'Abdu'l-Bahá personally, I pleaded with her to share with me stories of her experiences with Him. She responded, "No, go away now, I'm going to pray."

So I said, "Okay. Let's pray," and I very quickly recited the 'Remover of Difficulties'.

Kathryn looked at me tenderly and lovingly and said again, "Jenabe, I'm going to pray."

Not one to be put off so easily, I said, "Okay. I'll go away and come back this evening and you can tell me about 'Abdu'l-Bahá."

"No," she said. "I told you I am going to pray."

"Wait a minute, it's only two o'clock in the afternoon. What time will you go to bed?" I asked.

"I usually go to bed around nine," she replied.

Up to this time in my life, the longest time I had ever spent in prayer was probably five or ten minutes, and this little old lady was going to pray for *seven* hours. I learned a very valuable lesson and have ever since prayed for longer periods. The first hour many things crowd into my mind. The second hour these thoughts clear away and the third hour I am immersed in an ocean of spirituality that is beyond description.

The remainder of that day Kathryn spent in prayer and meditation, and early the following morning, in spite of the terrific cold and the icy streets, that fearless warrior of Bahá'u'lláh ventured forth in quest of those ever-ready and waiting souls.

Her first contact was with a man so loaded with bundles that he was unable to see Kathryn, and had almost knocked her down as he came rushing out of a door. He began apologizing profusely, but Kathryn — ever alert and ready — assured him she was quite all right, but if he would come tomorrow at three to her hotel for tea, she would give him a message and share with him the most wonderful news! They then exchanged names and addresses. He hurried on and she proceeded on down the street. This was the pattern of her day. The librarian, elevator boy, waitress, man on the corner — whoever caught her eye, smiled at her or spoke, received an invitation.

At the end of the day I truly loved this little, old and frail lady. She was so devoted and so self-sacrificing. I said to her, "Kathryn, tomorrow, when none of these people come, please don't be disappointed."

Those blue eyes again shot fire and she responded, "Don't you worry! Don't you worry! Bahá'u'lláh guides me. Bahá'u'lláh guides me."

I am sure she was guided, for on the following day at three, her little room was filled to overflowing. People sat on the bed, the chair, leaned against the wall or the sink and wherever else they would fit. Kathryn and I, with hearts throbbing with the fire of the love of God, besought the Almighty for assistance. Kathryn then unfolded the story of the coming of Bahá'u'lláh in one of the most spiritual talks I have ever heard. You could hear water drip in the sink when she finished, her audience was so awed and overcome.

Little Kathryn, never one to lose an advantage, went through the room serving tea. She then passed out books, giving one or two people a copy of *Bahá'u'lláh and the New Era*, others *Gleanings from the Writings of Bahá'u'lláh*, telling them they could come back to learn more, and arranging her deepening classes. Some said they were too busy and others were not interested. Kathryn thanked them for coming and let them out. Later, I mentioned that it might be possible, with more tact, to bring these uninterested individuals to the Cause of God. Her clear reply was, "I don't have time. I don't have time!"

How often do we attempt to pick and choose? "Oh, wouldn't so-and-so make a lovely Bahá'í", we say, and subsequently dissipate our time and energies on those who have turned themselves completely away from the face of God. Kathryn put the words of Bahá'u'lláh into action – if they refuse, pray for them that God might graciously aid them. Suffice it to say, by the end of six weeks that angel with the fiery blue eyes had brought in and deepened nine new souls, raising our community to fifteen.

One other lesson I learned from this eternal sister of mine was the secret of teaching while still maintaining that individual investigation of the truth so vital to our real spiritual development. She would have one of her students read and discuss a passage and if she felt that they had found the essence, she would move on to the next reading. However, if they missed something vital, after the discussion she would gently say, "Now, couldn't it possibly mean . . . ?", thus lovingly guiding them to the pearl of wisdom. Had someone come into her class unexpectedly, he would have thought *she* was the student, and those seekers after truth, the teachers.

Kathryn was a golden light in my life and in my spiritual development. Even until her earthly end, she continued to guide and inspire us, her children. Her last letter to us explained that she had fallen and broken her back, and while she was in the hospital one of the doctors had accepted the Faith and others were studying, and wasn't it wonderful how Bahá'u'lláh was using her! Such devotion cannot but cause rivers of tears to be shed, for this handmaiden, in great pain, thought only of the advancement of the Cause of God.

CHAPTER

4

ABOUT THIS TIME I had one of the deep spiritual experiences that have affected my entire life. Word had been received in the American Bahá'í community that the door was once again open for pilgrims to visit the World Center in Haifa – and Shoghi Effendi was extending an invitation. Upon receipt of this information, my soul was seized with such longing as is indescribable. However, still firmly attached to my material civilization, I assumed that it was financially impossible to accept such an invitation. Oh, if I had only had the detachment I now possess, I would have had the privilege to meet and know Shoghi Effendi, but I denied myself. The average American goes into debt for house, car, appliances, vacations and everything else, but for the most precious and wholly spiritual gift of all – he cannot afford it! My heart and soul said, "Go, even if you must walk," but my mind and satanic fancy argued, "No, don't go, for you cannot afford to." In those early days my mind ruled my heart, but such was my inner agitation and longing that I soon could think of nothing else but Haifa, Bahjí, 'Akká and Shoghi Effendi. My work began to suffer, my nights were sleepless, and I even lost my appetite — and so I wasted away in my valley of inner longing.

However, my deliverance was at hand. We had hosted an especially beautiful Nineteen Day Feast in our home and the friends had left. My wife and children were asleep. As I sat up, once again reading *The Seven Valleys*, I soon became so enamored with that heavenly book that for the first time in many days, my agitation of heart was stilled, and a tranquility pervaded my soul, the like of which I had never known. The very air became charged with peace and nearness to God. Finally, having quenched my thirst at the fountain of life, I put down the book and retired to bed. No sooner had my head hit the pillow than I was in the Holy Land. I fully realized that my body was in Great Falls lying upon its bed but my spirit, flying free, had accomplished what the body refused to do.

The room I was in appeared to be of concrete, with a window on my left and another window straight ahead. The window on my left had a very low, wide ledge and upon this ledge was lying the Blessed Beauty, Bahá'u'lláh. How I prayed, but still He lay with His back to me. Then, in my dream, I went out of the room to tell Shoghi Effendi. He said, "You go right back in there and pray for someone other than yourself." This time the Ancient of Days was facing me and the reality of prayer set aflame my entire being as I prayed for others with complete abandon. That beautiful face was beyond description, but most extraordinary were the eyes. Now, for the first time in my life, I knew adoration, devotion and selflessness. As my prayer raced heavenward, such heavenly singing was heard surrounding me that the roof of that room opened up and I felt myself ascending. I realized my body was upon the bed in Great Falls, but it seemed to me that not only my spirit, but also my body was rising. Upon this realization, the vision ended and I came back so abruptly that I shook the bed and awakened my wife. I closed my eyes and cried out, "Oh Bahá'u'lláh, please come back and I vow that my body and self will not be allowed to interfere." But the vision had ended, and I fell into a deep and dreamless sleep.

Having made this spiritual pilgrimage, my heart was at rest, my soul content. I fully realize that such spiritual experiences are quite common among the friends and I also know that the meaning of these experiences is for the heart of the recipient, but I have recorded this incident here because in my life it has been a guiding light, and will always remain a confirmation of the nearness of God.

My job took me and my family briefly to Oklahoma, where we assisted in the Bahá'í work in Oklahoma City and Tulsa. One thing I learned here is that the problem of prejudice is a very sharp two-edged sword: not only is the white edge used upon the black, but also the black edge upon the white. Both sides can cut and wound a human heart with equal severity. Equality of race is built on mutual trust, mutual love, mutual respect and mutual understanding. This does not mean that we, as Bahá'ís, must wait for these qualities; it means that even with lacerated and bleeding hearts we must persevere in the battle, using our limitless ocean of love to establish that equality so necessary to world unity. We, the lovers of the one true God, must build into the world through our actions, the supreme edifice of unity.

From Oklahoma we went directly to the great, never-to-be-forgotten World Conference in Chicago, where we were privileged to meet Amatu'l-Bahá Rúhíyyih Khánum, Hand of the Cause of God and the wife of the Guardian, and be anointed by her own hand on behalf of Shoghi Effendi. The Mother Temple of the West was being dedicated, and how happy I was remembering that as a child I had saved my pennies to help build it as a gift to humanity, that all men might enter arm in arm, heart to heart, in adoration of the One Supreme God. That conference also saw the launch of that child of the Guardian's, the world-encircling Ten Year Crusade. In discussion with Dorothy Baker, and later on the platform in front of the conference, my wife and I dedicated ourselves to the accomplishment (God willing) of all the tasks given us by our Guardian in that crusade.

One night my wife and I consulted to see which of us would go to hear Amatu'l-Bahá, and which would stay with the children at the hotel. Of course, I 'won' the hotel.

That evening, when all was quiet, I made up my mind that I would take advantage of this opportunity, and, as a fitting reward for missing the meeting, I would pick the best place in the entire world to pioneer. I laid the world map out on the hotel room floor and carefully eliminated all the undesirable spots, finally ending with Tonga Island in the South Pacific as my selection: a climate semi-tropical, a queen, a radio station (possible work), and relatively free of insects. What more could we want? When Elaine came in later that evening, she readily agreed to go with me to Tonga.

One other experience happened at the conference that was very extraordinary. I was crossing the hall, intent on my destination, when beloved Hand of the Cause of God, Tarázu'lláh Samandarí, whom I had never seen before and who was in consultation with a large crowd, stepped away from them, intercepted me and kissed me on both cheeks. Then, without a word, he returned to his discussion. Only later did I learn his identity.

When we returned to Great Falls, we began disposing of our worldly possessions. Even the wedding gifts went. I entered into a state of great agitation at this time, because after meditating and praying about Tonga, my heart came to the conclusion that it wanted to go where it could best serve the Cause of God and humanity, not just end up at a beautiful spot. How I longed to sit down and write about my problems to the beloved Guardian, but Rúhíyyih Khánum had closed that door firmly when she said on stage, "Don't you dare write to Shoghi Effendi and ask if that means you; it means you! Just pick a place and GO!"

I lay awake nights, twisting and turning in my bed, crying out from the depths of my soul for that promised divine guidance. Papers were processed for visas, and so on, and were finalized and ready to mail. Tonga was our apparent destiny. Truly, God is a prayer-hearing, prayer-answering God! Just as we were leaving the house to mail those final papers, the phone rang and it was our beloved Dorothy Baker, from the National Spiritual Assembly, calling long distance to advise me that they had just received a message from the Guardian requesting them to fill three goals at once. Two were easily filled but the third was impossible, so it seemed: the Aleutian Island goal.

Oh God, my God, what tongue can voice my thanks to Thee! Is this not abundant proof of the nearness of God to us, His helpless creatures? Was not every doubt and longing of my heart answered, even down to our receiving direction from Shoghi Effendi, our valiant Commander-in-Chief? I know this could be construed by doubters as one of the mere accidents of life, but read on, dear reader, for the odds against such 'chances' at critical times increases every time the divine promise of assistance is offered. After many years of active service to this Cause of God, I can, without the slightest reservation concerning Bahá'u'lláh's promises, state that verily, God keepeth His promises.

Our directions were confirmed, our employment terminated, our junk sold or abandoned to those who desired it . . . Day followed agonizing day, but our third child, who was now overdue, was quite comfortable in his little nest beneath his mother's heart. Finally the doctor decided it was long enough, and sent Elaine to the hospital to induce labor. Within a week of the birth of our third son, we were off to Butte to say a last farewell to my mother. Somehow I knew I would not see her again on this mortal plane, and my final prophetic words to that dearest of persons was, "God willing, I will be with you again in heaven."

CHAPTER

5

WITH ONE SON four years old, one two years old, and the third only four weeks old, we started out for Alaska and then on to the Aleutians. The most significant event on that trip was yet another evidence of divine assistance.

Bahá'u'lláh states that if we should arise to aid His Cause, the concourse on high and angels, rank upon rank, will rush to our aid. One night after we had bounced over the rocks and ruts of the Alcan Highway and were deep into the Yukon Territory, hundreds of miles from civilization, we pitched our little six by six foot tent. The rush of a mountain stream, the beautiful light of a full moon, the sighing of the breeze through the pines; the babies all sound asleep — at first as I lay on the hard ground and listened to the unfamiliar night sounds, I realized how completely we had turned to God and how from now on, He alone would be our security. Gone forever was the false security of the material world. The tent began to be filled up with the Divine Concourse. Such warmth, such love, such tenderness and compassion was felt on every side that

each rock, shrub and bush around that little tent rever-
berated with peace, peace, peace; and praise and
glorification of God. This time, I was not in a state of
semi-consciousness, but fully awake and with both
outer and inner faculties turned to the realm of light.
Words fail me in describing that most glorious confirmation. Every atom of my being was set afire with the
love of God, and that overwhelming feeling of
nearness to God has not left me for one moment since
that time. My continual prayer is, "Oh my God, keep
me firm and steadfast in Thy path; I can conceive of no
greater hell than the most burning fire of separating
myself from this nearness. Praise be to God, the Lord
of all the Worlds."

Upon our arrival in Anchorage, we pounded the
streets and found that there were no jobs available in
the Aleutians, that the islands were destitute and that
the natives who lived there, for the most part, were on
government relief or worked at the government sealing
operation in the Pribiloff Islands. Every door was
firmly closed in our faces, yet we took the tools of
courage and determination to fulfill God's Will, and
tore the door right off the hinges.

We know God's Will. I have here before me as I
write, a shelf full of the Holy Writings — every word,
every sentence and every page filled with the Will of
our Beloved for us, His children. Please God, may we
achieve, in accordance with our preordained capacities,
complete and faithful obedience to Your decree.
During the Crusade we had Shoghi Effendi and now
we have the plans of our Universal House of Justice for
guidance. My eternal prayer for you, each and every
one, is that you will arise with love and wisdom to

fulfill your heart's desires, in this heavenly realm of complete and pure obedience.

Elaine and I learned that the only forms of transportation to the Aleutians were by air or by a ten-day boat trip. First, I went to the owner of the airlines. He was very blunt and tried to discourage me. He said, "Leave those people alone; they have their religion."

I replied, "Praise be to God that they do. If they really have a religion, you can be assured that we would be the last ones in the world to try to take it away from them. Our purpose is to teach them the truth of what they have and the unity with what others possess."

Suffice it to say that we did not get passage on his airline due to our lack of funds and the owner's desire to keep us away.

That left the monthly mail boat. Off we went to Seward to meet this boat and, if at all possible, book passage. I boarded the *M. V. Garland* with the prayer the 'Remover of Difficulties' pulsating through me. "Captain," I said, "I want to book passage for myself, my wife and three young sons, to Unalaska, in the Aleutians."

"What in God's name do you want to go out there for?" he asked.

"That is it exactly," I replied, "God's name." I went on to give him the news of the dawning of the new light of God, Bahá'u'lláh, and our desire to share this with the native people of the Aleutians.

The Captain was very much impressed and said, "I like your spirit, young man, and I'll tell you what I am going to do. I am going to take you, your family and all your luggage out to Unalaska for $120, and next month I'm going to bring you all back for nothing." I might add that eight years later he stopped at the local Hazíratu'l-Quds in Unalaska for literature.

On the trip out, through some of the worlds most ferocious seas, we all became sick. I slept on the mess hall table and Elaine and the children slept in the liquor closet for the first part of the journey, until a room was made available.

Word of our arrival had preceded us to Unalaska (our own virgin goal of the Ten Year Crusade) via the newspapers, and we were met with a form of prejudice and hate we had never before experienced. So that you may better understand the welcome we received, I would like to share with you some of the background I have discovered over many years, concerning the history and legends of these beloved Aleut people.

From the beginning that has no beginning to the end that has no end, divine favor and mercy has surrounded God's creatures, and Bahá'u'lláh's words, *I have been with you always*, show that no people are left unattended by the direction and guidance of the All-Merciful. In the Old Testament it was written to those dwelling in the Holy Land at that time, that they must build an ark, and within the ark were to be placed The Tablets of God. Then, as the story goes, if the people would care for the ark and those Tablets, God would be their God and they would be His people. As man has evolved, his spiritual needs have changed; it is apparent that in those days, man needed something he could feel, see and touch, and God in His infinite wisdom, fulfilled those needs.

On the other side of the world, we picked up the old Aleut legend. All the islands from Unimak west were devoid of trees, yet the legend says that one great tree grew on the island of Umnak in the city that today is called Nikolski. Sometime, God came to these children of the kingdom and told them that this was His Tree, and if they would take care of it and protect it, He would be their God and they would be His people. Surely no one can read this without acknowledging *All are His servants and all abide by His bidding.*

Such was the devotion of these people toward God that their greatest aspiration in life was to visit this spot in their lifetime and circle round the Tree, giving praise and thanks to God . . . I might add that these true and fervent lovers of God would come from as far away as Kodiak, which was and is covered with trees, and traverse, with their precious families, 600 miles of the foulest seas and weather imaginable. Their only transportation was a tiny skin boat, and their only resource the sea itself, as they made that pilgrimage to the Tree of their heart's desire. What devotion, what love, what sacrifice!

Now we leave legend and come to history. The invaders, in their quest for furs, gold and wealth, swept eastward and found the Aleuts, who were brave, fearless, hard workers and sons of the sea, to be ideal slaves to aid in the rich harvest of fur seals and sea otters. With no knowledge of the Aleut language, customs or legends, the invaders saw these blessed people prostrating themselves around a tree, and the clergy of the invaders arbitrarily gave the order for destroying this 'Pagan God.' The Tree was not easily severed, for those spiritual giants defended it with spear and knife against the guns of the invaders. Finally, with the island soaked in blood, in the name of that tender-hearted Christ who so loved mankind He could not endure the least pain and heartache in anyone, the evil of the invaders was achieved and the tree fell. History says that every male Aleut on Unalaska Island over the age of seven was killed. Gracious God, by what stretch of the imagination could anyone condemn a child of seven for paganism?

If Christ had come Himself to this distant land to find these children had been led astray, what would have been the actions of this divine King? Even the most elementary knowledge of His Book suffices to show that He, with love, tenderness, wisdom and kindness, would have led them to the ocean of life. Do we not have the example of Bahá'u'lláh Himself, when He came upon the dervish who claimed to be cooking and eating God? What more base thought can ever be imagined? Bahá'u'lláh dismounted from His horse, lovingly embraced this dervish, and with complete love and tenderness led this errant soul to a true understanding of the unknowable nature of God. So completely did He win his heart that the dervish, abandoning his pot and fire, followed after Bahá'u'lláh singing praise, thanks, and glorification to the One True God. Such also was the way of Christ, and so must be the way of those who desire to follow after Him in His name.

The cutting of the tree did not terminate the pilgrimage of the Aleuts. Still those pure and stout-hearted men came, and throwing themselves at the tree stump, they would cry out to God, asking His forgiveness since they had not been obedient in protecting His trust. The invaders built a church near the spot, and over the tree stump they built a small house with no openings. They would tell the little children that inside the building were evil spirits that had already caught their parents and that therefore they must not go near it or the evil spirit would get them also. There were no windows or doors, in order to keep the evil spirits inside.

Now, with the entrance of the Cause of God into this dead and desolate area, what tremendous spiritual potential would we find hidden in these beautiful hearts, if their past devotion could be used as an example? Like a flower that begins to open, they will surely one day add their sweet fragrance to God's divine garden.

CHAPTER
6

FROM LEGEND AND HISTORY, back to my story. Our first duty was to send a telegram to Shoghi Effendi giving the time and date of our arrival, to which he replied, "Loving prayers surrounding you." From darkness we are finally coming out into the light! Complete confusion reigned in the Unalaska telegraph office when, in this isolated corner of the world, we sent the first international wire, and received a reply all the way from Israel!

Upon our arrival, I was met on the dock by a local missionary with the question, "Are you a Christian gentleman?", to which I replied, "Oh yes, and a Muhammadan and Buddhist gentleman also." My remark upset this worthy person no end and he told the people that we had come to take Christ away, and were not Christians. What is a Christian? I believe he is one who loves and adores the reality of Christ and strives with all his heart to follow Christ's teachings, which are the teachings of God. With complete love and tenderness, Bahá'u'lláh has brought us to the fountain of Christian teachings, and adoration of that most blessed Spirit of God, Jesus Christ. I went several times to this missionary and pleaded that together we might show the harmony, love and basic unity of the religion of God. He insisted that I was only intent upon his flock which was, at the most, three or four persons. He finally let me understand that I was not welcome at his church, not even to pray with them. God knows that I made every effort to establish love, harmony and unity between us and received in return the worst type of slander for my efforts. I suffered in silence, and turned my heart and soul to God, the best of helpers. The missionary's life came to an end when he went out in his small boat one beautiful, calm, clear day and his boat turned over and he drowned. This occurred after we had been in the Aleutians for four years.

The slander and hate that bore in upon us is even now impossible to describe. We did, however, find a house to rent, and set about trying to make a permanent position for ourselves in the Aleutians. I obtained a job as bouncer and garbage-dumper at the local saloon, and Elaine washed the beer glasses, but I quit the job at once when the missionary accused me of taking the job away from a poor native.

Thus we went into our first winter with the local mayor as our only friend, no work or prospects of any kind, no income, a house that was well ventilated, and through which the wind blew continually. I spent my days fishing and my wife cared for the children, chopping driftwood for the stove, and doing the laundry as best she could by hand.

Surprisingly, during this time we were more gloriously happy than we dreamed possible, attaining a beautiful intimacy and companionship. In the evenings when the babies were in bed, how hard we prayed together and how we learned the value and reality of true spiritual marriage.

Let me share a secret with you of successful marriage. As my wife says, the greatest psychiatrist or marriage counselor is the prayer book. A great wisdom is one I discovered from 'Abdu'l-Bahá. As we all know, according to the teachings of Bahá'u'lláh, when a mistake has been made it must be rectified, so divorce is permitted. 'Abdu'l-Bahá, in elucidating this, said that after a one-year period of separation, if love is not re-established, divorce is allowed, but *God have mercy upon the one who is at fault*. If an honest mistake has been made and two people are incompatible, then no one is at fault and neither will fear the malediction of God.

Let's take a typical real-life situation: my wife is upset and clobbers me over the head with the frying pan (which upsets me slightly) and I storm out of the house, slamming the door, which she locks behind me. Before I've gone a block from the house the statement, *God have mercy upon the one who is at fault* hits my heart. I vow that if there is to be trouble in this marriage it will not be my fault, so I turn back to the house. My wife has also had these same thoughts, and has already unlocked the door. I ask you, how can anyone have problems in a marriage when both partners love and fear God completely and both go more than half-way in order to solve their problems? Praise and thanks be to God for the wisdom of 'Abdu'l-Bahá!

Ye say ye believe and not be tested? Or again, *With fire we test the gold.* If the gold did not go through the purification of the fire, the impurities would never be burned away and the pure, radiant gold of the human heart would never become manifest. The winter closed in that year of BE 109–110 (1954) with a fierceness that the ten following years never equaled. I had built a small, twelve-foot skiff for securing seafood, but as the elemental forces of nature crashed and thundered, the boat was useless. By the end of our second month in the Aleutians we had snow up to the eaves of the house. On hooks in the living room, I had hung an old, rotten fish net which I tore out, re-sewed and tore out. Between the living room and kitchen we hung a blanket to divert what heat our little wood stove produced into the kitchen for my wife and the babies. Such was the bitter cold blown into the living room by the unrelenting wind that within fifteen minutes, I would be forced to abandon my net sewing and retreat into the warmth of the kitchen to thaw out. In this manner my net was hung.

During this period, we had written to the Guardian, but not told him we were out of money and just about out of food, with absolutely no prospects of work. Yet in that unerring, divinely guided atmosphere, Shoghi Effendi was able to read through the lines of our correspondence and reach around the world (not only to us but to others from whom I have heard many stories), and pick us up, dust us off, sending us the encouragement and guidance we so sorely needed. Such was the case at this time. We received a letter from Amatu'l-Bahá, signed by Shoghi Effendi, telling us we should accept help from the National Spiritual Assembly of the United States. After much deep, soul-searching prayer, we wrote back pleading that we not be allowed to take from a fund which we longed to give to. To us this was unthinkable, and with hearts overflowing with love and gratitude, we begged that we might make this sacrifice as an everlasting example to our Bahá'í family on the home front, that they might follow in our footsteps and forever wipe out that deficit which was continually clouding the glorious record of achievement.

The subsistence problem moved swiftly to a climax. One day Elaine (who walks the spiritual path with practical feet) advised me that we were out of money, almost out of food, and that it would be impossible to last out the winter. We sat together that night in such a spirit of prayer and meditation that even remembering it today fills my soul with delight. Our decision was to begin the following day by going on rations. As the children had no say in the matter, we would feed them normally, but as for Elaine and me, our food would be rationed to make it last until spring.

How can I describe the joy and happiness of that night? My soul sang and my thoughts, as I dropped off to sleep, were that now at last I would be able to sacrifice something for my Beloved. Even as I write this many years later, this desire to sacrifice has gone unfulfilled and I can truthfully say it is impossible to sacrifice for the Cause of God. By just making the effort, myriads of oceans are your recompense. I speak from experience and not just high or idealistic words. So it was – as we slept, the storm died down and after three long, unrelenting months we had a dead calm.

I was awakened in the morning by a pounding on the door, and upon answering, found the superintendent of Standard Oil Company from the adjacent island of Amaknak (better known as Dutch Harbor) standing there. He explained that the storm had taken out the power lines. He understood that I was an electrical engineer and asked if I would like a job fixing them. I immediately accepted, asked Elaine to put on breakfast — and so ended our starvation rations before they ever began!

I have yet to go hungry for the Cause of God. In all honesty, I had to explain to the superintendent that an electronics engineer who designed computer circuits was not a lineman, but I was sure I could do the job . . . which I did, even if at first I put the pole spurs on backwards, never having seen a pair before.

One job led to another on Dutch Harbor. Finally it was spring and I had work digging a ditch completely across Amaknak Island to bury the power lines. Also in the spring, the fishing boats headed north and it seemed as though every boat that came into our bay had something broken down that needed fixing. My fame as a repairman spread on the radio waves, and soon I had more work than I could possibly handle. That first autumn was our lowest spot on the economic ladder and from then on it was upward.

By far the greatest gift of all during those early months was the assurance from Amatu'l-Bahá that the spirit which animated us had made the Guardian happy. For me there has never been any greater achievement in my life; and praise be to God, the best of helpers, we had been obedient to the last Will of 'Abdu'l-Bahá and had touched, with a moment of happiness, the great heart of Shoghi Effendi, whose radiant heartbeat was in harmony with the Cause of God. When the victories came for his Cause he was happy, and when word of division, defeat, or negative actions of the believers reached him, he would become so unhappy that he would be unable to eat. My heart cries out to each Bahá'í now and in the future: Let us, each and every one, strive with all the diligence of our hearts and souls to really, truly, be Bahá'ís in every thought and action. Then, not only will we never further stain the snow-white robe of the Blessed Perfection, but will fill with happiness and delight that unique emblem of God, Shoghi Effendi, in the realm of glory that he now occupies.

One other incident shows how our Guardian always had his finger on the pulse of the world. We had, after prayer and consultation, decided upon an open proclamation to the fifty families who lived in our corner of the earth. No one, besides my wife and myself, was aware of this decision. Once more, out of the blue, came a letter from Shoghi Effendi, saying, *Do not openly proclaim the message of God in this place; when you have confidence in them and they have confidence in you, then slowly confirm them in the Cause of God.* Oh, what praise and thanksgiving we send to God for His radiant gift to us of the wisdom of our Guardian. My heart throbs with wonder and astonishment, for now, looking back, I can honestly say that had we openly proclaimed His message at that time, we would have been driven from the island and the door would have been closed for a long time. Yet, through the intervention and wisdom of our most beloved Shoghi Effendi, the door remained open and through the years our roots went deep. The hate gave way to tolerance, the tolerance gave way to acceptance and finally all gave way to mutual love and respect. Even today, these Aleut people are very slowly being confirmed in the Cause of God.

CHAPTER

7

THAT SUMMER of BE 111 (1955) was one of fierce activity. We needed better housing for the family, and since we had sailed forth only for the Cause of God, we thought, why not build a Bahá'í Center to live in, which in the future could serve the Faith? We bought a piece of land for $150 (the best in town) and three old army buildings for $2.50 each, and went to work. We knew that in order to stay for the duration of the Ten Year Crusade we must also build a permanent job, so we started a fish cannery. With thirty-five fathoms of net, the twelve-foot skiff, an old abandoned military site that we homesteaded, and with my wife and I as the sole employees, we made a beginning.

Our day would start at 4:00 a.m. and end at 10:00 or 10:30 p.m. It worked as follows: I would be out of bed at 4:00, into the twelve-foot skiff, and out to sea. I would find a school of fish, surround them with the net and haul them into the shore; then load them into the skiff and return to the cannery. In the meantime, Elaine dressed the children, cleaned the cabin and washed diapers and laundry in water that she hauled from the

river. While I carried the salmon into the cannery on
my back, she started breakfast. After we ate, I began
cleaning the fish while Elaine did the dishes and got
the children off to the field to pick coal.

Sending the children, then aged five, three and
one, to pick coal, was far better than having a baby-
sitter. When the army left the islands following the
war, they had bulldozed surplus coal into the ground,
so the children had the job of scratching around and
rooting out those lumps. You can well imagine how
much coal picking got done — usually the boys played
tag and built sand castles. A bucket that could have
been filled in ten minutes would take them all day, but
they always had the job in front of them, so they never
wandered very far from the bucket!

With the children taken care of, Elaine would join
me in the cannery and begin cutting and inserting the
fish into cans. Then, using an exhaust box to secure a
vacuum, a hand seamer and a pressure cooker, I would
finish the job. The first year we canned forty-two
cases, or 2016 cans of salmon, and so an industry was
born. I also took electronics jobs, and every spare dime
we earned was put into the Bahá'í Center and the
cannery.

Using our first bathroom at the cannery was a rather
amusing and interesting experience. Near the cannery,
way out over the ocean, was an old dock. In order to
save time and effort, I conceived the idea of cutting a
hole in the dock and building an outhouse. It really was
grand — there was no door, so one could look out across
the bay at the mountains and at times see whales,
dolphins and sea lions feeding and swimming in the
ocean. I also put in two holes in order to accommodate

two children at once, thus giving Elaine a break. In theory, view, and so on, it was all very nice, but let me now describe how it worked in practice! First, the two seats were a failure because of the windy climate, and after the first time Elaine used my great masterpiece, I was out there with a board and hammer nailing up the second hole. It seemed that the wind blowing over the water and dock caused an updraft, so that when the paper was disposed down one hole, it would come flying out the other side, past your head and out the doorway. As to the view, no one ever had time to enjoy it, for the wind would pick up the cold spray from the Bering Sea, giving us the only toilet in the world with a free shower thrown in. I will never forget the sight of my spouse, with a tiny tot by each hand, sprinting like mad for the outhouse, her head thrown back, springing into the wind. She would try to beat the sudden urge of a child, running like a gazelle of the desert, and I am sure, had not the primitive eventually given way to the modern, she would have been able to enter the Olympics as a sprinter and hold her own against all comers.

In the year BE 112 (1956), my wife was with child and the nearest medical facilities were 800 miles away in Anchorage. We had neither doctors nor nurses available, and my concern for the safety of my wife was heightened by the fact that on the three previous pregnancies, we always had the best help available. At about the same time I was offered a position in my former line of work in the electronics field, at a choice of Alaskan cities in Anchorage, Kodiak, or Fairbanks. This offer seemed to be an answer to our prayers, for not only would transportation, housing, and medical aid be furnished but also a good salary with an additional twenty-five percent cost of living allowance. To secure this, all that was necessary was to sign a contract for one year.

The Guardian had asked us not, under any ordinary conditions, to abandon our post, but in the event of circumstances beyond our control we should write, giving him the details. In conformity with this request, I sat down and poured out my heart, explaining the lack of money for sending my wife out, the apparent open door for employment, and that in a year we would come back with enough money really to put down our roots. Had I been able to look ahead, I would assuredly never have written that letter. I was absolutely certain that Shoghi Effendi would tell us to leave (with his blessings), but praise and thanks be to God, he did not. The essence of his reply was that he would prefer that we stay. My heart was instantly set at rest by his reply and Elaine was pleased, for she wanted the baby to be born by natural childbirth.

I am content with the will of God – what boundless oceans of happiness lie hidden within the depths of this contentment! Alas, only those of us who have completely and without any reservations submerged ourselves in this ocean can know of the treasures that lie hidden in its depths. No written or spoken word of mine can ever hope remotely to touch any other heart with this reality, and my pen can only add, in complete awe, adoration and love for the bounties of God, "Glory, Glory, Glory be to Thee." No praise is, or can ever be, adequate in gratitude for the least of His infinite bestowals, much less for the greater gift of contentment with His will and pleasure.

Feeling completely unworthy to unfold to you, dear reader, a description of the nearness of God, I considered at this point terminating this work and destroying the manuscript. If all the sticks in creation were turned into pens, all the oceans into ink, and all mankind into writers, still we would be unable to elucidate even a remote glimmer of this reality. Yet, powerless and incapable as I am, a force I can neither explain nor understand compels me to continue, for the story must be told. I cherish the hope that you will pray for me and overlook my shortcomings, that happily I might in some small way bring happiness and a glimmer of light into your hearts. If this can be achieved, then the purpose of my labor will be fulfilled.

To assist in the childbirth, we secured the services of a native midwife who was far more competent than many doctors. The respect and admiration of our neighbors was now complete. Elaine was going to have her baby as they did. At this period in the history of mankind, the miracle of new life had been relegated to a cold, sterile, efficient hospital routine, as the experience of the births of my three sons had proved. When my wife had informed me she was in labor, I had responded by rushing her to the hospital. Then she was taken into the maw of this grand edifice, to what, I knew not. But if the doctor and staff could not assist her, I certainly couldn't, so I was left in a waiting room to read, sleep or what have you, ignorant of the tremendous drama going on. Later a nurse would appear, informing me that I had a son, whom I could see through a large plate glass window if I cared to. My wife was usually resting, and I was told I would be able to see her on the morrow.

This time I was with my wife. I wouldn't let her out of my sight. She clung to my hand. How desperately she needed me, and I realized how desperately I needed her. Never before had my heart plunged to the depths it now reached; such love and tenderness and above all, compassion, did I feel for my wife. We had a most beautiful marriage, physical and spiritual, and here was the fruition of that marriage. Had this delivery not terminated when it did, I surely would have fainted, for my heart could hold no more.

The baby arrived in the water sac. My wife assured me that this was the easiest birth of any of our children. God gave us our baby girl, whom we named for the tale in *Seven Valleys* in which the lover searches everywhere that haply he might find his beloved. Laylí (the one of pure spirit) came into our lives as a gift for our obedience. Within a few minutes of her birth I held her in my hands. I looked into that precious, tiny face, and because of her birth in the water sac, she was beautiful. Such a prayer of thanks and gratitude welled up in my heart, and from the very depths of my soul I pleaded with my God that He would accept her as a true handmaiden to the Cause of God. No sooner did this prayer leave my heart than that tiny face became illumined before my very eyes and that radiant smile was confirmation that I had been heard, although I knew that she still must make the effort and win for herself this predestined glory.

I then carried my wife, whom I now loved more completely and tenderly than ever, into her own bed and gave to her our new and precious bundle of pure spirit of light. I never dreamed I could love my wife more, but over the years my love has deepened and the completion is still not in sight.

Once, as I described all this to a very close Bahá'í friend, he said, "Caldwell, I don't understand this! My wife has a baby, she just has a baby — but when your wife has a baby, you have a spiritual experience!" I have since thought about his remark. Had I been able to look ahead to this tremendous, earth-shaking spiritual experience, I never would have petitioned the Guardian for permission to leave. Not only was the child of my obedience born, but I would not exchange for the entire world and all of its gold the precious moments of my life that I lived during that delivery.

At this point I would like to relate a couple of incidents concerning our children, which occurred during our stay in Unalaska.

My Laylí Roshan, at the age of about two years, as we sat over dinner one evening talking about God, said, "Daddy, I know where God is."

I replied, "Sweetheart, Daddy would like to know."

"I'm afraid."

"Don't be afraid; Daddy will go with you."

At this, she climbed down from her chair, and taking my hand, led me into the main room, pointed at 'Abdu'l-Bahá's picture and said, "That's God."

Our eldest boy (at about five years) was looking out the window one day watching two small boats racing across the bay, and enthusiastically shouted, "Wow! Look at the human race!"

Year followed year. The cannery grew larger and larger, and in the year 112 (1956–7) we also completed the Bahá'í Center. When our Guardian heard of this he advised us this would fulfill an auxiliary goal of the Ten Year Crusade. The year in which the Center was completed, an angel of God paid us a visit and dedicated it to the service of humanity. I am speaking of Florence Mayberry, whom I met first in Oklahoma. Our lives have come together from time to time since, and each encounter for me is like coming into contact with a brilliant star and fills my heart with light and warmth. From my acquaintance with her I can say every act and thought of hers is dedicated to service in the Cause of our Beloved. I would willingly lay down my life in her path. Another important event of this period was the rendering into the old, original Aleut of the prayer, 'Blessed is the Spot,' translated by an Aleut, Simeon Pletnikoff. Simeon later became a Bahá'í. This achievement was also listed by the Guardian as an auxiliary goal of the Ten Year Crusade.

CHAPTER
8

OUR GUARDIAN, looking ahead in his letter of 30 June 1952, warned the Bahá'ís of the world of *the ordeal of temporary separation from the heart and nerve-center of their Faith which future unforeseeable disturbances may impose upon them* . . . We, the Bahá'ís of the world, had direct and infallible guidance from the very inception of God's new revelation. From when His Holiness the Báb, closeted with Mullá Husayn, first revealed Himself, until that fateful day in BE 113 (5 November 1957) when our beloved, lion-hearted, self-sacrificing commander-in-chief, Shoghi Effendi, winged his flight to the realms above, we were never alone. First the Báb, then Bahá'u'lláh, followed by the Master, and finally the Guardian were always there to guide us. I well remember how, when we had received this message, we all contemplated what it could mean. Oh! What earthquake can compare with the shock of this loss! How completely we were cut off and how unforeseeable it was! Yes, we still had the Guardianship that is destined to carry us at least another 900 years. Yes, we still had the plans of immediate action. Yes, thank God, we had those nominated Hands of the Cause of God, those stout-hearted generals trained at the very hand of Shoghi Effendi. Yet, from BE 113 to 119 (1957–1963) – for six long, excruciating years – that temporary separation from the heart of our faith as forewarned by Shoghi Effendi himself, was in truth, for some of us a separation so complete as to be unimaginable. Our heart finally began to beat again in BE 119 (1963), with the formation of the first Universal House of Justice, when the true link with divine infallibility was once again re-established.

Upon receipt of the wire about the passing of Shoghi Effendi, and subsequently his last messages, my wife and I vowed that the best tribute we could pay to him would be to carry out in every last detail his hopes, his pleas and his final wishes for us. After much study it was apparent that we were doing all we could possibly do, yet after sincere prayer and meditation, we settled on one thing more. In addressing the American Bahá'í community, the Guardian had made the appeal to the Bahá'ís to recapture that pioneering spirit which had sent us forth on his glorious Crusade. We decided that I would go to the United States and travel the length and breadth of that land with the sole purpose of helping my precious Bahá'í family there recapture this spirit.

One does not have to arise and go to some foreign land to have the pioneering spirit. This is a very simple and very easily attained station. The recipe is: place the Cause of God first, before everything else. That's it! One could write books about pioneering, and still it would come down to that one simple proposition. First, above all else, must come the Cause of God.

Now let us examine this proposition. You do not have to give up your family, nor is it necessary to give up anything else. In fact, your family, your job, and so on become more precious, since everything is based upon that very firm foundation, the Cause of God. The pioneering spirit is not a place, but an attitude, a relationship with our God. I have known so-called pioneers who have gone to distant lands, only to return home disillusioned and heart-sick, for they did not venture forth first for the Cause of God. Other pioneers, who only moved to a nearby town, have become so changed and filled with the love, wonder and power of God that when I converse with them I feel as if I have conversed with heavenly angels.

I left on my teaching trip, leaving my precious wife to hold the fort at home. Since we had been spending every penny on our Bahá'í Center or canning business, we had little money, but as Bahá'u'lláh says, *Put your whole trust and confidence in God.* I used what money I could secure to buy a round-trip ticket to Seattle. When I arrived in Anchorage, the Bahá'ís arranged teaching work for me in that city. We had not breathed a word to any soul about our straitened financial condition and once more had stoutly refused any aid from the United States Bahá'í Fund. Despite this, a lovely Bahá'í lady approached me and insisted that, due to an uncontrollable urge she could not explain, she must help me financially. *God aideth whomsoever He willeth; all praise be to God, the Lord of the Worlds!* I will not go into detail about this trip as I have already recorded it elsewhere. Suffice it to say that I used her money to buy an old car and a credit card. With a heart overflowing with the love of God, my wife helping from Unalaska and myself on the road, we paid a bountiful tribute to our departed Guardian. From that trip alone we learned later of quite a number of souls who recaptured that pioneering spirit and went out in the final phase of the Ten Year Crusade.

On another teaching trip in BE 115 (1959), I traveled throughout Alaska and all of Western Canada in response to a suggestion by the Hands of the Cause of God in the Holy Land. On this trip I gave special attention to the Indians and also to the Queen Charlotte Islands. I terminated this trip as a teacher in the Geyserville, California Bahá'í Summer School.

The cannery continued to grow during these years, and we were able to hire all the local people who wanted to work, operating on an almost year-round basis.

We had planned, as far back as the year BE 109 (1953) at that great conference in Chicago, to attend, at the completion of the Crusade, the World Conference to be held in Baghdád. The location had been changed to London, but I am afraid we were very poor savers. I figured out that if we saved as much money beginning in BE 119 (1963), the year of the conference, as we did during the entire Ten Year Crusade, it would take us thirty-one years to pay for our transportation. With the North American, African, Australian and German Temples to be built, Temple land to purchase in Alaska, the Alaskan Fund, the World Center, and so on, it seems that whatever money did not go into our business or local Bahá'í Center, our conscience dictated should go to our beloved Faith.

My wife (practical feet) and I (spiritual path) no longer brooded over these matters. We decided to make the trip, and so naturally we took our four children and flew to London. I contacted various airlines until we found one that was willing to give us our tickets on a 'fly now, pay later' plan. Thus, I was able to attend three historic conferences: the first at Chicago in BE 109 (1953). The second I managed to get to only because I wished to give something additional to the memory of our Guardian and the National Spiritual Assembly gave me an itinerary that allowed me to be in Chicago in BE 114 (1958) — my heart overflows with gratitude for this blessing — and of course, in BE 119 (1963), I was in London.

On our first night in London I had a strange and moving experience. When it is noon in Unalaska, it is night-time in London. My family adjusted very well to the time change and soon all were sound asleep in the hotel, but my body would not cooperate. In the middle of the night, I was still wide awake. As I lay upon my bed I was seized by an urge I could not ignore, to get up, get dressed and go across London to the Royal Hotel. Although my mind argued that this was pure folly since all the Bahá'ís at the Royal Hotel would be in bed by now, my heart ruled supreme. Consequently, at 2:30 in the morning I arrived by taxi at the hotel and, as my mind had foretold, all were sound asleep. I went into the lobby, and except for a few night-lights near the desk, all was very dark and quiet, but it was a joy to me just to sit in a hotel realizing that almost all the tenants were lovers of Bahá'u'lláh.

One of the bell-boys came up and asked me if I was one of those Bahá'ís, and when I assured him that I was, he asked if I could explain the very queer experience he was having. It seemed that no matter which floor he would stop at, he would see a very dignified man with a white beard and cream-colored robes walking the halls of the hotel. I explained that there were many people from various parts of the world and possibly he had seen different men dressed in similar fashion. I also explained that, as with myself, the time changes could have caused some others to be quite wakeful. But he insisted that it was always the same man.

He soon forgot his strange experience as we conversed and I shared with him the life-giving waters of the Cause of Bahá'u'lláh. He called the other bell-hop over and they both sat on the carpet at my feet. Together we tasted the wine of astonishment, and our pure and intimate conversation was only interrupted once when the beautiful, spiritual lad went to the kitchen to bring back some tea and crumpets. We continued talking until the time the underground began operating, and as I left, walking down the nearly deserted streets of London towards the underground station, the young man stood in the street. For several blocks I could see him watching me go, and when I looked back he would wave. I believe that if I had given him an invitation to come with me, he would have abandoned his position at the hotel and gone with me to the ends of the earth, such was the tenderness and love of God that touched our hearts that night. I have often marveled at how strange and fortunate it was to have such a bounty on my very first night in London – the hotel was filled with Bahá'ís yet I was called across the city for the heavenly feast of sharing the message of Bahá'u'lláh.

While in London I lived in heaven, and I knew not if I ate or slept. On every side was my spiritual family and every one I came into contact with had a heart like mine, throbbing with the love of God. The high point of London, for me, was when Amatu'l-Bahá, with feeling, tenderness and love nobody else could have matched, brought to us the reality of our Guardian. With what compassion did we raise our voices along with those of our African brothers, to help ease her heart, which she so willingly lacerated in order to bring us close to him. However, every moment of the conference was a precious gift that will be a memory cherished for the rest of my life.

CHAPTER
9

WE RETURNED TO UNALASKA after the World Jubilee in London. The cannery had grown from our original forty-two cases per year to a capacity of 4000 cases per month, with an operational season year-round instead of only two months in the summer. Our main product had changed from salmon to the world-famous king crab.

A restlessness began to creep into my soul at this time. I felt that we had done all we could for the Aleutian Islands and the Faith of God — the people all had work now, all were aware of our Faith, and literature had been distributed not only in Unalaska but to the islands of Akutan and Nikolski. However, my roots had gone down so deeply that it seemed impossible to break free . . . like the heavenly bird described by Bahá'u'lláh, which soars on the wings of detachment and nearness to God, then descends into the mire and clay to satisfy its hunger, and with sullied wings is unable to resume its flight. I never had any purpose save service to God and humanity in this, our pioneering post, and never in the entire ten years had I let slip that pioneering spirit – first must come the Cause of God – which dominated our lives. Then it happened.

Everything was running very smoothly, although in a business such as ours, we were always in debt. For example, we would can $100,000 worth of crab, ship it to Seattle, and upon presentation of warehouse receipts would receive $70,000 advance on the future sale of the product. Eventually we would, after sale and costs, receive the additional $30,000 or whatever was left. Shortly after one such shipment, however, instead of a check we received word that the bank had refused the advance. To iron out the difficulties, I kissed my family goodbye, closed the cannery, and left for Seattle, descending into that black and ruinous pit Bahá'u'lláh so vividly describes. In Seattle every door was closed. It appeared that we had taken away some very good accounts from the million-dollar fish monopolies and, since business is business, it had been decided by them that we must go. I concluded that as I owed over $30,000 to my fishermen alone, it would be best to sell at cost and clear out. Again the competition was ahead of me and had just put 100,000 cases of crab on the market at fifty cents under cost. Of course, all these companies had to do was raise the price of their fruit or vegetables a few pennies a case to recoup their loss on the crab. But alas for us, we had only the crab, and faced bankruptcy.

At night I would go to bed and, instead of having a heart burning with the love of God, I was preoccupied with those sordid and worthless problems of life, and in the morning instead of, *I have wakened in Thy shelter, Oh my God*, it was, "Oh God, how can I pay my fishermen?" I could lock the cannery door and leave, except that I had tremendous responsibilities to others. I had told my wife I would be gone a week and it now stretched out into six months. I had a vivid glimpse of the reality of hell, and only an infinitely merciful God could deliver me from its flames. Totally immersed in the muck of materialism, I was swept into the vortex of a raging river like a small chip of wood. As it drew near to the time of the Fast I decided I was doing no good in Seattle, and since the Fast is a very special family time, I returned to my island. As the winter of desolation must give way to the reality and warmth of the new spring, so the spirit of God began to revive my drooping soul, as I turned to the healing waters of obedience to God. I am sure that only His tender love and compassion could have lifted me out of this slough of heedlessness.

As the Fast progressed, I began slowly, and then more rapidly, to advance once more into that realm of God from which I had descended. One day, while at complete peace and contentment, the revelation was born upon my spirit, *God doeth whatsoever He willeth*. Oh, what joy and relief permeated my being! My actions had been those of someone trying to play God. Oh God! My God, have mercy upon me! God is All-Knowing and All-Wise. In His infinite wisdom He decided whether these children must return to their former state of poverty for their own best interest. Possibly this poverty would allow us to leave and go forward on the Nine Year Plan. Was not my primary concern due to a tender love for these Aleut people? In any event God doeth whatsoever He willeth, all are His servants and all abide by His bidding.

After Naw-Rúz that year, I left home for Seattle again, completely submerged in the inner reality of these thoughts. Upon my arrival in Seattle, I did not contact the banks, brokers or wholesalers but instead called my Bahá'í friends and offered them my services for the weekend. On Friday I spoke at the Seattle Bahá'í Center and the meeting was indeed a heavenly one.

Upon returning to my hotel that night, news of the great Alaskan earthquake was being announced on television. The reports stated that the Aleutian Islands had ceased to exist. Although my most precious family was alone on one of those tiny islands, my first cry was neither one of anguish nor remorse, but complete contentment with God's will and pleasure, followed by a soul-stirring prayer for my family's protection and advancement, whether still in this world or in our Abhá Kingdom. Of course, as it turned out, the radio and television announcements were greatly exaggerated, and the islands were completely untouched. My wife had loaded many of the townspeople into our company's bus and driven them to the hills; but my family decided that they would rather drown in the tidal wave than freeze to death on the mountain, and had returned to our home.

This great earthquake lasted only three minutes, but in those three minutes every problem we had was completely solved. The companies that were intent upon our destruction lost every canning plant they had in Alaska. On Monday, the brokers and wholesalers fell over themselves to purchase my pack at full price. Another company that had lost its plant contacted me and arrangements were made to lease our business to them, thus freeing me for further service to the Cause of God and insuring continued employment for my beloved Aleuts. Within the week, I was returning to Unalaska for my family.

I am sure, as in the story of the birth of our little girl, some will say, "There was just an earthquake, but Caldwell has a spiritual experience." Be that as it may, if every atom of my being were turned to the most eloquent thanksgiving, my thanks would still be wholly inadequate to express what is due my Beloved for the least of His tokens.

CHAPTER

10

T O LIVE IN THE MIDST of civilization and yet
remain aloof from its evil influence is not an easy
task. The changeover of management at our cannery
necessitated my working in the company's Seattle office
for a year. We did not live in Seattle, faithful to our
Guardian's request for only fifteen Bahá'ís in a city.
Instead we moved to Edmonds, where we were needed
to maintain their Local Spiritual Assembly, and I
commuted to my job. Of all the assemblies I had known
and worked with, I can honestly say that the Local
Spiritual Assembly in Edmonds, Washington came the
nearest to being a truly Spiritual Assembly. Love, union,
harmony and always the best interests of the Cause of
God were the guiding lights of its honored members. I
do not want to leave my reader with the impression that
these lovers of the One True God were always a peaceful
Assembly – no, indeed they were not. Often the clash of
differing opinions was a dramatic one, with lightning,
sparks and fire, with each and every person always,
without reservation, voicing his or her opinion. Yet all
thought, meditation, and prayer were aimed directly at

the shining star of service to the Cause of God. The year we spent with them will always remain a very beautiful and tender memory.

Here we were in a strange land, after eleven years in the Aleutians, and of course we had no contacts. I could not see us, in that short period of a year, becoming friends with many people and giving them the life-giving water of the divine teachings. So I conceived the idea, after much prayer, of running an advertisement in the newspaper under the personal column, stating, "If you are not satisfied with your answers regarding religion, please call . . ." This newspaper had a circulation of over 300,000 and the advertisement was successful beyond our wildest dreams. One does not realize the number of people who have deep and soul-searching questions they would like to ask, and now a door was opened, in the atmosphere of anonymity, in which they could seek, yet fear no embarrassment. A few were anxious for further contact, so firesides were arranged in their homes, but the phone rang incessantly and my wife and I really made up for lost time giving the message day and night. We had a few cranks and a few jokers of course, but even the ones who called as a matter of fun became interested once we had joked with them a little and got into the heart of the message. The cost was negligible and only the future will adequately measure its effect, but for my own part, any one of a number of callers would have been sufficient for all the time and money spent on the project.

I will cite one case in particular as an example. When I answered the telephone, a woman was in tears. Through her sobs, she explained that she had just returned from the graveyard where she had buried her husband. She had come home to a big, empty house and, all alone, did not know where to turn. Then she remembered seeing our ad. What heart-rending anguish she suffered! I reached across the city on that telephone line and comforted that broken heart. I first set her heart at ease about where her husband was by using 'Abdu'l-Bahá's fine example of the garden, and God, the gardener, the All-Knowing, All-Wise Gardener who knows the exact time to transplant a tender plant into the sun from its shady corner. With infinite tenderness and love He does this, yet to us plants left in the garden of life, we do not have the wisdom of God and cry out in our separation, "Oh why did God uproot this most tender plant?" As I talked, my heart filled with a tender love and compassion for this sister I did not know and could not see. Her sobs slowly gave way to calm and certitude. Although I did not even mention Bahá'u'lláh or the Cause of God, I was able to touch her wounded and broken heart with this divine medicine when it was most urgently needed. How I thank God that I was there where I was needed most.

At this same time, our Local Spiritual Assembly in Edmonds launched a stupendous proclamation aimed at bringing the Faith of God to the attention of one million people in the greater Seattle area. I received the bounty of being the coordinator for the entire area, and so was privileged to attend Assembly meetings almost every night, sharing with these angels of God our hopes, our plans, and instilling in their blessed hearts enthusiasm for our project. Such love, such unity of purpose and such a financial response!

Driving forty or fifty miles home at night, I would be overcome with wonder and astonishment at the force inherent in this Cause of Bahá'u'lláh. Potentially, we Bahá'ís have the power to overcome the combined forces of all mankind, and the key that will release this latent power is the love, unity and whole-hearted cooperation of all the friends. In this effort, all inter-community barriers were destroyed and even one or two communities who at first did not care to become involved were eventually swept into the feverish activity of the proclamation. The Bahá'ís of the entire area, some for the first time, got a glimpse of the worldwide character of our Faith. I pray fervently that they will not allow themselves to be returned to that lethargy of provincialism from which they emerged and will promote the Faith wherever the destiny of God will place them – neighborhood, community, city, state, country and world. United, we Bahá'ís have a lever strong enough to lift the world completely free of its foundation, but as a lever, it requires us all to be pulling in the same direction. If one pulls and another pushes, the precious efforts will be canceled and rendered fruitless. Love, love; unity, unity; peace, peace!

The climax of this effort was a large meeting in the Seattle Playhouse, with our speaker none other than Florence Mayberry. But alas, I was destined not to be present for this grand culmination of a project on which we had labored so diligently. We had received word from Haifa that our long-dreamed-of pilgrimage was finally to be realized. Upon receipt of the letter from the World Center, we had just $5 in the bank, as every penny and dime we could get had gone into our proclamation. But undaunted, we began the 'fly now, pay later' plan again and were off to the land of our heart's desire.

CHAPTER
11

I FULLY REALIZE THE IMPOSSIBILITY of conveying to another heart anything but the crudest idea of the reality of the pilgrimage. I had heard a great many pilgrim reports before I went, and still remained completely unaware of the true reality. Although we live in a world of many dimensions, it is an impossibility, even using slides, movies and tape recorders, to convey to others the spirit of the pilgrimage. The first thing that struck me profoundly upon my arrival in Haifa was that idealistic forces were unified and harmonized in all their dimensions — the sound of birds singing and insects chirping, the faint fragrance of the gardens, the rustle of the breeze both heavenly and natural kissing the foliage, the spiritual forces in vibration, all tuned together like a heavenly orchestra.

We met the Hands of the Cause of God residing at that time in Haifa — Paul Haney, 'Alí-Akbar Furútan, Mr. Faizí, and for a few hours one afternoon we saw Amatu'l-Bahá. It is not my intention to take you step by step through this heaven of heavens, but only to set down my impressions. At the Shrine of the Báb and

'Abdu'l-Bahá, I prostrated myself in the presence of God and emptied my heart of all its burdens. At about 3:00 a.m. the morning of our proclamation, which would be 6:00 p.m. in Seattle, I arose and went to the shrine. There, oblivious of all except the nearness of God, wrapped in the atmosphere of prayer, I did what I could to help make our proclamation successful. As I raised my voice in prayer, it seemed to ascend, reverberate and spiral into that heaven of reality and, for the first time in my life, I felt in the very presence of my Beloved. When I said, "Oh God, my God", the reverberations resounded, "Yes, my child". At about 5:30, Elaine joined me, and together at that Holy of Holies we prayed, first one then the other, alternating. The outside door was closed and the peace and quiet of pre-dawn was complete, but as we prayed a very warm, tender, gentle, loving breeze (not of this world) fanned across us and the outer manifestation of *the divine breezes wafted over them'* set a fire aglow in our hearts. This again was a confirmation of our complete spiritual marriage, as together we tasted the same divine fruit.

My first impression of Bahjí was . . . peace. I had been in the wilderness of Canada and the isolation of the Aleutians, where the stillness can be heard when it is quiet, and I thought I had a vague idea of the meaning of peace. Yet the first glimmer of its true meaning was not given to me in those spots of worldly isolation, but in Israel, with civilization on the march swirling around with us in its very midst, in the holiest spot on earth. As I walked through the garden, every atom, shrub, rock and blade of grass about me resounded to the acclamation of peace and glorification of God, and my heart swelled with gratitude to Him that at least now those sanctified remains of the Blessed Perfection were granted a peace He had not been allowed while He walked this earthly plane. However, as I entered the center of adoration, the full realization dawned on me that it was not as I had felt. The very reason for the emanation of that peace were those blessed remains themselves. Gracious God, there is no end to the giving of the Ancient of Days: even in His realm of glory He continues to give and wafts His bounty upon us. Only for us, the children of men, does He give His all, wanting only our peace, our happiness, our glory and exultation. I offer my soul in complete realization of the magnitude of this offer, as a ransom for the troubles that fell upon Him at our hands while on His earth.

My pilgrimage was now building to a climax, and as I stood beyond the moat and looked up to that tiny window in the Most Great Prison, my heart went out to that early believer who, with failing eyesight, had walked from Persia to catch a glimpse of the white handkerchief of Bahá'u'lláh and then, at last, was unable to achieve even that.

I was completely unprepared for what happened at the Most Great Prison. At the cell of Bahá'u'lláh I removed my shoes. Paul Haney opened the door and I stepped into the cell. The impact was more than I could stand and my heart shattered into a thousand bits. To begin with, the cell, in every detail, was the room of my vision of twelve years past, when I had seen Bahá'u'lláh face to face. Added to this, I had been studying the teachings of Bahá'u'lláh for over thirty years and knew that every page, every line, every word and every letter of His teachings was filled with such love, such tenderness and such compassion that it was beyond minds to grasp, or hearts to understand. For Him to have been subjected to such cruelty, as I said, was more than my poor heart could stand. If tears were able to wash away any of the stains on the snow-white robe of Bahá'u'lláh, such a flood was released from my heart that I alone could have returned the robe to God, pure, white and stainless.

I was allowed, by my selfless brother Paul Haney, to remain alone a few moments with the fragments of my broken heart. I prostrated myself once more in the same spot as I had in my dream, and vowed that only by my complete dedication to His Cause to the point of laying down my life and giving my last breath in service to His Will, could my broken heart be mended. I pray to God with all the sincerity of my poor inadequate human heart that He will grant me the privilege of fulfilling my vows made in that sacred spot.

From the prison, we proceeded to the House of 'Abbúd where Bahá'u'lláh had been confined on the upper floor for five and a half years. I walked out on the balcony where Bahá'u'lláh used to go for air and exercise. As I leaned upon the balustrade I thought, "Every inch of this has been blessed by the Supreme Manifestation of God." How I envied the dust that was blessed by the touch of the Hand of God! I then recalled those closing passages in the *Epistle to the Son of the Wolf* about 'Akká and I began to count the forty waves as they beat against the sea wall. As I reached the count of the fortieth wave, it felt as though the last wave did not stop, but came right up over the balcony, descending over my head, washing and rewashing me in that blessed water. I felt as new and clean as if at that moment I had stepped from my mother's womb into the world. Once more I cried out to God from the very depths of my soul that He give me His protection and keep me safe from the mistakes and sins of the future. Verily, God doeth whatsoever He willeth. First Bahá'u'lláh, then 'Abdu'l Bahá and Shoghi Effendi likened our World Center to the heart of the world. The heart is a living, pulsating reality and we flow into it from the distant parts of the body, filled with all our impurities. Then, cleaned, oxygenated, reinvigorated — we are pumped back into the extremities of the world to bring this life-giving nourishment to the dying body of mankind. Yes, truly, this is the heart of the world.

On the final day of pilgrimage I walked with my wife in the gardens of Haifa and prophetically told her we were going to have another child. She replied all with her wifely ardor, "Not me! I have all the children I want and I'm too old to be bearing any more." However, almost one year to the day later, my wife had our fifth child, our daughter Zarrin Taj born in Mexico. This child was God-sent to my wife, giving a focus to her life in that country.

The last time I entered the Shrine of the Báb, the spiritual forces that pulsated around my head and in my soul were so powerful that I could barely stand to enter. I feel that as man evolves spiritually, he will be unable to enter those holy of holies — not because anyone says he cannot, but because the spiritual power emanating from them will be more than his soul can bear.

CHAPTER
12

FROM THE LAND of my heart's desire, Haifa, we returned to Seattle where my first bounty was the gift of the presence, once again, of my dearly beloved and cherished sister, Florence Mayberry. I was able to spend several weeks in her blessed presence. Often I would take her to a meeting (her schedule was monumental) and my heart would shed tears of anguish for her physical condition. But she always managed to reach out and draw on that supreme, promised assistance, and like a girl in her early teens, shared the water of life with those with whom she came in contact.

I will share with you one small incident, which is in reality a large incident, for it will give you, dear reader, a better glimpse of this radiant soul that has so captivated my heart.

Florence, as an Auxiliary Board Member, was not only charged with propagation of the Faith but also with its protection. Therefore, she had the task of meeting with a certain individual who had withdrawn from the Faith and was now actively engaged in undermining the community by sowing seeds of doubt and suspicion in the hearts of the friends and contacts. We first met with one of the seekers this woman had contacted and, with tenderness and love, Florence won him completely to the Cause of our Beloved. We then went to the home of the woman who was on the edge of becoming a Covenant-Breaker. Florence met this woman with such tenderness and compassion that it is almost impossible to describe. She took the woman into her arms and lovingly kissed her. Then in a spirit of love, those two sat hand in hand upon the sofa and truly had a heart-to-heart talk. Such wisdom, such tact, such understanding and above all — such love! Every question of this misguided one was met honestly, frankly and sincerely. A person completely dead and cold spiritually could not have helped but be guided back to the straight path by Florence's words. Our wayward sister, with tears streaming from her eyes, embraced Florence and requested her name be put back on the voting list. The story of the prodigal son now took on a new significance for me as I plumbed its inner secret, for this reunion gave us more happiness than had the acceptance of the Faith by a new believer a few hours previously.

Florence and I could sense the impetus from our earlier proclamation slowly dying in the hearts of the friends and did our best to encourage and revive the spirit. Florence talked about the purpose of selling. Once you have your product well advertised and on the market, once everyone knows of it and is beginning to buy, you do not give up production. But alas, like a lamp that has run out of oil, the ardor of the friends had cooled. After Florence left, almost every believer told me they had personal problems and advised me in no uncertain terms that they did not want to be pushed.

One Sunday my heart directed me a number of miles away to the home of a beautiful Bahá'í family and, as we talked, my Bahá'í friend pointed out that there were over fifteen tribes of Indians right in our local area. I instantly realized why my heart had brought me to his home. We began immediately to make plans. My energy and resources, the wings of my spirit, now took on a new direction. I went to both of the University of Seattle libraries and spent several weeks on research into the customs and history of the local tribes. I found that west of the mountains in Washington there were nineteen distinct tribes, which I felt was significant, nineteen being the number of a complete *Váhid*. We worked with the blessings of the Indian Teaching Committee.

I was determined to use the direct approach that was so effective in Yucatan, Central and South America. We needed the names of the chiefs, or headmen of each tribe, in order to contact them first, and thus try to reach the people through their leaders. I learned that the Indian Agency in Everett had just such a list and I prayed that God would put it into our hands. I had visions of going to the agent, and discovering that he had an aversion to all religious movements on the reservations. With many misgivings I drove to Everett, praying all the way, saying the ever-powerful 'Tablet of Ahmad', and 'Remover of Difficulties'. Upon arriving at the office of the Indian Agency, I was met by an Indian boy, and asked to see the agent. He explained that the agent was at one of the reservations for the day. I told the young man what

I desired and he, wanting to be helpful, opened up a book and showed me the list, which certainly was impressive and very long. When he realized that I intended to copy it, he opened a file, drew out a copy of the list and gave it to me. God doeth whatsoever He chooseth, and all are His servants! Home I went, armed with not only a list for those tribes in western Washington but also for the entire northwest, plus a heart singing with gratitude to my Beloved!

The Indian teaching activity was really something. Letters were written to all the leaders asking for an appointment that we might share with them the glad tidings of God's latest revelation. At that critical time, I received a request from the National Office of the United States, to make a trip to California and Oregon in order to help save Local Spiritual Assemblies that were in jeopardy. As it was already the first of April, this did not give me much time, but off I went, interrupting other activities. All the weak Local Assemblies were saved with the exception of one that was down to five believers.

Upon my return to Washington, we had received only one response from the reservations, with an appointment scheduled several weeks away. After much prayer, meditation and consultation we decided to go to one of the reservations and personally contact the Indians if at all possible. If this failed, we would make personal contact with the chief on the reservation. Since the nearest and most easily accessible place was the Tualip Reservation near Marysville, Washington, this became my goal.

After a soul-stirring period of prayer, and with a heart overflowing with love, I made my way to the

Tualip, deciding on the way that when I arrived in town, I would park the car, stroll through town and give the message to everyone I met. This I proceeded to do, but as I walked from one end of town to the other and returned to my car I did not meet a single, solitary person — Indian or white. *All are His servants and all abide by His bidding.* I walked to the beach, sat on a piece of driftwood, said the 'Tablet of Aḥmad', and then returned to Edmonds.

The next day I went back, right to the Agency office and asked for the chief. When I was shown into his office and introduced, I came right to the point and said, "A new and Divine Messenger of God has appeared upon the earth with a special message for your people." Had I hit this gentleman over the head I could not have given him a greater shock. His mouth dropped open and he looked at me long and hard. Finally, when he recovered his composure, he advised me that the best way to disseminate my message would be to go to the various priests and preachers on the reservation and they would give it to his people. Back to the driftwood on the beach and my prayers for assistance!

At this point, I began to feel that perhaps I was not the one to reach these souls. However, on Friday we had a teaching conference in Seattle, and at this conference, an Indian Bahá'í from Yakima, who had gone with Florence Mayberry to the Yakima Reservation east of the mountains, got up and made an urgent appeal for assistance on follow-up on the reservation. I had made up my mind not to go east of the mountains. Why should I drive 150 miles when we already had nineteen reservations in our immediate area? But after her desperate appeal, I waited for someone to respond. None did, so not being one to let a person down who wished to serve the Cause of God, I arose and offered her my services. We made arrangements and within the week I picked up this Indian lady. She then asked if I would mind taking along another Indian friend from Tacoma, who turned out to be a full-blooded Tualip! Praise and glory be to God, who had allowed me to follow my heart in its service to the Cause of God!

As my Bahá'í sister and I began to talk, this Tualip gentleman boldly asserted that he was a very contented and happy Catholic. I told him that was wonderful, and went on talking animatedly with my friend. Our Tualip Indian said nothing for the first fifty miles, but when we stopped for lunch he was asking questions a mile a minute. Then, for the next fifty miles, we submerged him completely in the ocean of God's love. By the time we reached Yakima and the reservation, our beautiful Tualip was so excited he could not sit still. Upon recognizing an Indian friend of his on the street, he requested me to stop the car. We had hardly come to a stop, when he bounded out, grabbed his friend's hand, and declared vigorously that a new Messenger of God had come. For the two days we spent on the reservation, this man proved himself a fearless warrior of Bahá'u'lláh and vigorously championed the Cause of God. On the three-hour trip back home he began to lay his plans for bringing his new-found Beloved to the Tualip people.

I had made my plans, but how vastly different were the results! This also proved to be the case with our first Tualip Bahá'í in the Cause of God. We made plans, and he and I received permission from the Indian

Council to have a Bahá'í picnic on the reservation. Our Tualip Bahá'í had picked the place that he knew the Indians would come to. Now, it so happened that the Local Spiritual Assembly that had this reservation as a goal made a visit to the reservation and decided that the spot we had chosen was not a proper place for such a dignified gathering, with friends coming from all over western Washington, because of the presence of outhouses, lack of a kitchen, dust, and so on. So these well-meaning friends, purely for the sake of the Cause and the welfare of the Bahá'ís that would come, changed the place by renting a very exclusive spot. Well, exclusive it was – only the Bahá'í guests came and no one from the reservation except our Tualip Bahá'í.

While the Bahá'ís enjoyed themselves, this Indian and I drove over to the spot previously deemed 'inadequate', and sure enough, the place was full of local Indians. I only tell this tragic incident of our Bahá'í picnic because I wish to make a point. The life-giving waters of the Cause of Bahá'u'lláh are for all humanity and are not exclusive. If we are ever to succeed in our task we must go to humanity with open arms and open hearts, and meet them wholeheartedly on their own ground, not on ours.

We met with those Indians who had given us the invitation, and although we did not win any new believers, we won some lifelong friends, and received special invitations to attend all their functions.

CHAPTER

13

AS AN ELECTED DELEGATE from our area to the National Convention, I was off to Chicago with Elaine. Here we were privileged to meet many new believers and were thrilled with the change and growth of our American Bahá'í community. We also met a friend who asked if I could make a trip through the South. I could not refuse service to a cause so close to my heart. The race riots and the terrible forces of negation were causing the blood of both Black and white to flow in the streets, as prophesied by 'Abdu'l-Bahá. I felt an obligation as a believer to go forth throughout that strife-torn country and demonstrate by deed and action that we, the Bahá'ís, were not only talkers but doers as well. At the convention, permission was finally granted by the National Spiritual Assembly to allow our family to respond to the request of our beloved Hand, Dr. Giachery, to serve in Mexico as pioneers.

After Convention, we returned to Seattle until the end of the school term, then said goodbye to each of those Bahá'ís in the north-western United States with whom we had worked so hard and whom we had grown to love so much.

The trip throughout the South lasted three months and was very fruitful in securing new declarations, and especially for demonstrating to all the real meaning of racial unity. We stayed many times right in the heart of the black districts, living in private homes, accepted and loved by all. We were threatened and cursed by the ignorant, but the feeling of spirituality among the Blacks of the South is a true and beautiful ray of light in an otherwise dark and disillusioned area. In one place we were the first whites ever to enter the black church, and were received with tenderness and love, and allowed to speak to their congregation. For three months, day in and day out, we strove with heart and soul as instructed by 'Abdu'l-Bahá, and finally on 12 Asma 121 (31 August 1965) we entered Mexico.

We were assigned by the National Spiritual Assembly of Mexico to the State of Oaxaca, since one of their goals of the Nine Year Plan was to have believers in every State of Mexico. Oaxaca is situated in the high sierras of Mexico, with the city and capital of the state, Oaxaca, lying in a valley nestled in these mountains. Oaxaca has the distinction of having the largest native Indian population of any state in North America, and after eleven years of pioneering in a community with only fifty families, it was heaven! Also, after eleven years of the foulest weather on earth, God allowed us the privilege of the kindest and gentlest climate possible.

'Abdu'l-Bahá has instructed the Bahá'ís that, before going to a country, one should become proficient in that language. Praise and glory be to the wisdom of

God – I have truly suffered by my disobedience. I could only say 'good morning' and 'good-bye' in Spanish when I entered the country. So, for four months, I worked day and night to master the language, and the words of Bahá'u'lláh, which have been the driving force of my life, kept me going. He said:

> *Night hath succeeded day, and day hath succeeded night, and the hours and moments of your lives have come and gone, and yet none of you hath, for one instant, consented to detach himself from that which perisheth. Bestir yourselves, that the brief moments that are still yours may not be dissipated and lost. Even as the swiftness of lightning your days shall pass, and your bodies shall be laid to rest beneath a canopy of dust. What can ye then achieve?* (Gleanings, p. 320)

I do not believe anyone with a sincere heart can read the foregoing and not be totally consumed with the inadequacy of time and the monumental tasks that lie immediately ahead.

At the end of four months I had mastered only the barest rudiments of the language. However, as I had learned so many years ago about putting one's trust wholly in God, once more I arose each dawn and went forth to the mountain that overlooks the city of Oaxaca and there communed with God in complete contentment with His holy will and pleasure. One of my first fruits and gifts from God, I received from my nine-year-old daughter. Most mornings she would tumble out of bed, groggy from her sleep, but eager to help her daddy, and would dress and go with me. God alone can know the joy and happiness that would pervade my soul as this pure spirit of light would sit close to me, and in her sweet and pure voice read prayers as we drove to the mountain. Then, as the light slowly illuminated the eastern heavens, she would join me in saying the 'Tablet of Ahmad', which she almost knew from memory. I pray God continually that this Crusade child of my obedience will continue to mature, keeping that purity and radiance of soul she now possesses.

One day I advised Elaine that I was going to Mexico City. She wanted to know what for, since we did not have the money for such a trip. I honestly did not know why, but she had learned (as I had) not to stand in my way or object to the prompting of my heart.

It so happened that a young girl from Venezuela, a Bahá'í for only a short time, was passing through Mexico City, and when I asked her if she would like to come to Oaxaca and help for a while, she was very enthusiastic. With the blessing of the National Spiritual Assembly of Mexico, the arrangements were made. Now I would have a voice, since this child of the Kingdom was bilingual. Oh God, my God, what tongue can voice my thanks to Thee! Once more those words, *God sufficeth all things* were abundantly manifested in my life.

Her name was Trina, and although new to the Faith, she had a wonderfully warm, loving and open heart so vital to the teaching of the Cause. She was to follow me to Oaxaca with some other friends by car the following week. What prayers of thanks filled my heart as I flew back home. I determined not to lose a precious moment, and upon my arrival in Oaxaca I turned toward that ever-present nearness to God that surrounds me. In that rarefied atmosphere of *God doeth whatsoever He willeth* and *He is the best of helpers*, I asked where we could begin. Although I have a poor memory for names, one *pueblo* (village) came into my heart like a neon light. Its name was Zoquiapan.

CHAPTER
14

I DID NOT EVEN KNOW where the *pueblo* of Zoquiapan was located, but by the second day after I had returned home, I was determined to go the following day and see what arrangements could be made there for Trina when she arrived. I learned, mostly from a local map, that Zoquiapan was about eight kilometers from the nearest road, which I judged to be about an hour and a half trip each way. The next morning I secured the aid of an American boy who had grown up in Oaxaca and spent his days roaming the high sierras near the city. He spoke English at home and Spanish everywhere else so I mistakenly thought he could translate for me as well as guide me to this village. I knew he was mentally backward but he had a fine spirit and, like all humanity, he just wanted to know that he was loved and needed.

At 11:00 the following morning we started off. Since the sun was high and warm and I expected to be back in Oaxaca by 6:00 that evening at the latest, I did not even take a sweater. That eight kilometers turned out to be the direction the crow flies and unfortunately

I was not equipped like a crow. In the first place, the road from the highway to the jumping off place was little more than a donkey trail, so I gave up and parked the car, reasoning that I would still be back there before dark. To make a long story short, we walked, and we walked, and then we walked some more. I was overweight and after the first eight kilometers I cursed my indulgence and vowed that I would, in the future, carry no more weight into those mountains than I absolutely needed.

About 6:00 p.m. we finally arrived at our destination, over three mountains and approximately twenty kilometers. One of my toenails had worked into my foot, my sock was filled with blood, and my crying muscles made every step unbearable. Reason attempted to take over from my heart, and I felt that it would be unthinkable to subject Trina to the terrible ordeal of coming in and going out of Zoquiapan. Now that I was there, however, I determined to give them the message, leave, and forget this village. The people were very, very suspicious. When they asked what I wanted, and I replied that I had come with a new message from God, the people would walk away. My guide, I discovered, knew only one language – English and Spanish were all the same to him. When I spoke in English, he answered in English and when someone else spoke in Spanish, he answered in Spanish, never realizing the difference.

So I stood all alone, save God, unfamiliar with the language, in an apparently hostile situation. I sat in a corner and in complete reliance and contentment with the will of God, repeated to myself the 'Remover of Difficulties'.

As I prayed, a drama unfolded that I would not
believe, had it not happened to me. A native entered,
looking as though he came straight out of a western
movie. He had on a big hat, six-gun, boots and all. On
his belt buckle in gold was the word *Policia* and even
with my limited Spanish I understood that. He asked
what I wanted and I again explained that I had come
with a new message from God. He rattled on, a mile a
minute. I understood nothing of what he said, and my
guide was useless as a translator. However, I caught one
word, 'identification'. I took out my Mexican Bahá'í
credentials. I do not believe he could read, as he only
glanced at them, then satisfied, handed them back. He
then turned to the boy. I found out later that this game
they play is an extortion racket, and he was after
money.

As the policeman talked to the boy, I could see the
consternation and fear in the poor lad's face. Finally, he
bolted out the door with the cop right behind. When I
saw the policeman drag out that formidable hog-leg of
a six-gun, I caught his hand and explained in the best
way I could that the boy was *loco en la cabeza* (crazy in
the head), which was all I could do with my Spanish.
The policeman shook me loose. In the meantime, the
lad had fallen into a water ditch and was soaking wet,
but he had long legs, and the cop had short ones. The
policeman began to shoot, but there were no bullets in
the gun, thank God. I started down the mountain but
my foot and sore muscles prevented me from making
much speed and, realizing I could be of no assistance, I
committed the lad to the care of God . . . and so left
the crazy cop chasing the crazy boy over the mountains. When I returned to the municipal building the

entire atmosphere had changed. The whole village had watched this affair with great merriment, and being a warm and generous people by nature, they felt a compassion for this poor gringo. Never in my life, up to this time, had I seen such a rapid change.

Quite a number of people now gathered around and in my halting Spanish I gave them the healing medicine of the love of Bahá'u'lláh. How eagerly they received it, their enthusiasm was overwhelming! Thank God my heart reasserted itself, and when they asked questions, I promised that in four days I would return with a *senorita* who would answer all of their questions.

By now it was totally dark and five or six people accompanied me up a hill to get some *tortillas* to eat. As we were returning to the municipal building, a young man stepped out in the road and said, "This is your home." The men accompanying me argued that sleeping arrangements had already been made elsewhere. However, this beautiful young man ignored them and looking directly at me, said once again, "*Esta es su casa.*" God doeth whatsoever He willeth. I thanked my other benefactors for their help and followed the young man into his house. Sitting completely at ease within, unharmed and safe, was the American lad who had accompanied me into the mountains.

I first sat with my host, then with his sisters, and gave them the message, then the father entered. Although very humble, he mirrored forth a quality and dignity not often encountered. He sat down and very gently said, "Tell me." After I had done the best I could, I promised them all I would be back that weekend with a translator. There could be no doubt of their sincerity, warmth and love. Finally, my host gave me his own bed, which consisted of a very short plank without bedding. The night got colder and colder and colder, yet my host's sister slept outside on a narrow bench, also without bedding. My muscles began to stiffen, and at about 2:00 a.m., I decided that if I remained another three and a half hours on that bed, I would turn to ice and would have to be pried off. I got up, went over and opened the door, and gazed at the biggest, most beautiful moon I had ever seen, which turned the night almost into day. Every star shone with a brilliance reserved only for those mountainous retreats. The boy and I hiked out toward the car by moonlight and kept warm by struggling up and down mountains.

By the weekend my foot had swollen and I had a very severe infection, but did not He say, *Make an effort for Us and in Our ways will we guide you?* I could not stand on my foot, and had soaked it in various remedies, even carved at it with my knife, all to no avail. Of course, I had made my return to the village provisional and I always do – 'Insha'llah' (God willing). I could still see every face in the village and many had said, "Oh! Will you really come back? If you will come to teach us about God, I will stay home from my work. I will wait for you." No, my heart would not let me disappoint those sincere hearts. How happy I was with this decision! Now I truly felt the day had come when God was about to let me sacrifice something in His pathway.

This time I drove the car to the very end of the road, which saved us seven kilometers but cost me $100 in damage to my vehicle. As Trina and I struggled up that first mountain, every step was pure agony. Finally, stout-hearted little Trina stood in the trail with a tear running down each cheek and said, "I can't, I can't, I can't." We sat down and said some prayers, then got up and struggled on. Upon reaching the summit of the mountain, truly one of the greatest miracles of my life took place. Trina again stopped, but this time with a face radiant and beaming with light she exclaimed, "Oh, oh, oh, what a heavenly place! I have never felt such a spiritual place. I feel as if God is with us, really with us." My own reaction was that now Bahá'u'lláh was walking with us, and once more I was denied the privilege of giving something to the Cause of God. Who is there among us who would not crawl on our hands and knees to have the bounty of walking with the Glory of God? With hearts filled with joy we went forth, singing the praises of God and sending Alláh'u'Abhás cascading over the mountains ahead of us. I felt no more pain, and though still on this physical earth, I had ascended into the heaven of heavens. I must have floated all the way to Zoquiapan, for I cannot recall walking.

We had six declarations in Zoquiapan that day, all in the family of my hosts from the previous visit. Our first Bahá'í, the daughter of the family, walked hand in hand with Trina quite some distance down the trail when we left. With exhausted bodies but joyous hearts, we made the long trek back to my car. As we ascended an extremely difficult mountain along the trail, there appeared a small adobe house. My body cried out for a little rest and I reasoned that surely this must be a Bahá'í home where those warriors of Bahá'u'lláh of today, and in the future, could rest as they come and go to Zoquiapan. I said to Trina, "Surely this is a Bahá'í home," and courageous little soldier that she was, Trina marched to the door with a cheery "*Buenas tardes.*"

The man who came out was a spiritually dead man. Only his innate courtesy suffered our intrusion, but as we were tired and Trina was enthusiastic, we sat and gave the message. This little man sat with lifeless eyes and closed ears. We learned that when he had lost his wife, all purpose in his life had drained away, and even his body was wasting away. He looked to be eighty years old. How my heart yearned over the poor, unfortunate one. At every pause or question, he would respond with, "*Si*" (yes) and although I knew he had heard and understood nothing, I did not interfere. I concluded that I had made a mistake in stopping at his home. Finally, as he had agreed with all Trina had said, she asked him if he would not like to be a Bahá'í also. Of course, as before, he said yes. When Trina asked him for his name, he showed the first sign of life and one could see the realization dawned on him that he had committed himself to something he knew nothing about. Only the words *All are His servants and all abide by His bidding* can explain why I held my peace and did not interfere. This will remain one of the mysteries of my life, for I feel it is important to make absolutely certain that one understands completely the reality of the coming of the Glory of God, Bahá'u'lláh. When a soul has accepted and truly believes in this reality, then surely he can be numbered as a true Bahá'í, for the following of *what His pen has revealed*, will in most cases come as naturally as new plants follow the spring rain.

The man explained that he could not read or write, but Trina told him that God wanted only his heart, and she would sign his card for him. So, very reluctantly, he gave Trina his name. My heart was so filled with tender love and compassion for this empty little man that I got up and lovingly took him into my arms, told him how much he was loved and needed, and now with us all, he could help build a new and beautiful world in the Cause of God. Then Trina warmly took his hand and welcomed him in the same spirit of love and tenderness into the Faith. For the first time since we had met him, he truly came alive and we witnessed the rebirth of a wonderful child of God. At these evidences of love and warmth he responded, "Wait a minute, just a minute, I really want to be a Bahá'í but that name I gave you is not my name. I want my real name on that piece of paper."

On our next visit this little man, with eyes shining, ran to embrace us on the trail. When I said, "Do you still really want to be a Bahá'í?", he answered us with, "Oh yes! and already I am telling my neighbors about God's new Messenger." On this second trip we presented him with a small Greatest Name, designed by some dedicated artist friends. He took it and lovingly kissed it, and assured us he would place it in his home in the most honored spot, with his Saint Guadalupe. His daughter-in-law, he explained, although she was supposed to read the prayers to him, read them herself instead, so he had to take his prayer book back.

Then we met his daughter-in-law Pascuala, in her ragged clothes, as she worked laboriously grinding her corn. I tasted from her the reality of sincerity in the love of God. She never just *mentioned* the word 'God'; every time she said it, she uttered it with such a love, respect, reverence and sincerity that I was thrilled from the soles of my feet to the top of my head. As tears rushed to my eyes I cried out in my soul, "Oh my God, I come as the teacher when truly I am the student. And who truly are the poor? Not this angel before me who lacks even the barest necessities of life – but we, of the world." I would most gladly give up everything else if I could but attain to that sincerity and purity cf spirit she inherently possessed. She explained how much she believed in Bahá'u'lláh and how she loved the prayers, yet she was afraid to sign her card because her husband would beat her. I told her not to worry; the card was only a symbol and only her belief and heart were important. I gave her a prayer book of her own. I wish that you, dear reader, could have experienced but a drop of this soul's love of God, for I am sure it would have been a revelation to you, as it was to me.

On our next visit, Pascuala explained that although she feared her husband, she feared God more and she insisted upon signing the card. Then she set about gathering her ragged clothing, advising us that now she was going to run away from home with us as she did not want her husband to beat her. Now, weren't we in a fine predicament? We lovingly told her about the importance of unity and especially family unity, that the purpose of the Cause of God is to unite people, not divide; so she stayed for God. We learned later that her husband not only did not beat her, but is now also a firm believer in Bahá'u'lláh.

In the spring it was necessary for me to go north on business and when I returned to Oaxaca, our little man's face had filled out, his step had a bounce and he now looked as if he were only thirty. With what love did he receive us! And amazement upon amazement, as we entered his house, lo and behold, Guadalupe was

gone and all alone was that beautiful Greatest Name on
his wall. At that time we had thirty-four Bahá'ís in the
pueblo of Zoquiapan and each one is a story like those
related above. We have had, as 'Abdu'l-Bahá promised,
people come to our door to declare themselves. In the
State of Oaxaca we had 125 declarations in about
twelve months of active teaching.

ONE DAY, out of a clear blue sky I advised Trina
that on the following day we would go to San
Jerónimo Taviche. We had never been there but, in
order to go, we were told we had to take a train. The
trip on the next day was uneventful and we did not even
meet anyone in the train with whom we could share the
bounty of God. Upon our arrival, we found no village,
only a train station, and the conductor advised us that
Taviche was about a half a kilometer down the trail but
we would not have time to visit the village as the train
only unloaded and returned immediately to Oaxaca. My
feelings were that I had chased the rainbow, and I went
off to play with the children while Trina talked to the
conductor. Little did I know the pot of gold we were to
discover at this rainbow's end. As we were once more
seated in the train, returning to Oaxaca, Trina said, "You
know what that conductor told me? He said there is no
one in the world who cares anything about the people in
Taviche."

There was nothing anyone could have said that
would have touched my heart so deeply, and I assured

Trina that we would return. If nothing else, we would tell these people that we loved them and that all the lovers of God in the world really, truly cared for them, although to do this would involve a fifteen-kilometer walk to get back to the highway where we could get a ride back to Oaxaca. Thus the die was cast, and a few days later we were once again on a train to Taviche. As we climbed up the path toward the village, Trina wanted to know how we could go about telling strangers that we loved them. I assured her it would be very easy, for God would guide us. *I lay all my affairs in Thy hand.* When we approached the town, Trina once again asked how we were going to begin. Never in my life had I had such sure and strong guidance, as I pointed to one building up ahead and told her we were going to start there.

We were met at the door by a very beautiful young man who seemed to be expecting us. He invited us in, gave us chairs and when we were seated, asked what we wanted. I responded that we had come to talk about God. He interrupted me, and said, "Just a moment; I am going to tell you why you are here. You have come to tell me about a new Messenger of God and to share with me His message." Both Trina and I were speechless. Not only did he accept immediately and spontaneously the person and the Cause of Bahá'u'lláh, but explained that he had been searching all his life for this. Being educated, he had studied a number of different sects and denominations but had never accepted any of them. He explained that the night before our arrival we appeared to him in a dream and he had been forewarned of our purpose and mission. Therefore, he stayed home from his work, cleaned up and waited for our arrival. Upon reading this, can any fair-minded person still deny the nearness of God?

Our new friend was called Efren and he pleaded for literature that he might know what his new-found Beloved desired him to do. We promised that on our return we would bring him some books. We then went through Taviche, but we met no other friends and never had we been received with such animosity as in this town. The hate and suspicion hung heavy in the air. With the victory of Efren warming our hearts and the fierce rays of the sun burning our bodies, we hiked out of Taviche.

We never saw Efren again. After a short illness of three days, he passed away. Five days before he became ill, we had been in the village and left the longed-for literature without seeing him, as he was working in his fields. He penned with his own hand on the fly leaf of each book, "Thanks be to God, the Lord of Eternity." His mother told us that some of his last words to her were that he was giving his life for the people of Taviche. The transformation of this town was almost instantaneous. The animosity changed overnight to a spirit of love and friendship and there were soon fifteen believers in Taviche, most of them from this man's family.

Many years ago while in Unalaska I made a very serious mistake. This was with the local children. When we first arrived the children were completely won to my heart. Yet I reasoned, erroneously, that it was best to win the parents first and the children later. Subsequently, a newly won believer in the Aleutians started children's classes and I helped. These children are some of those who are today accepting the Faith.

Suddenly one day I realized that those same children who had followed me through the streets, called me Daddy and held my hand, were now fifteen to twenty-four years old. I vowed that never again would I make this mistake. Now I take the children first, and while they color and play, if I have time I conduct the adult classes. What a joy this is! In the town of Santo Domingo Tomaltepec my class grew to over 150 children. Every night as I returned from the villages I raised my arms to heaven and cried, "Oh God, my God, increase my astonishment at thee!"

In one village there were only two believers, both old women, who could neither read nor write. How I worried for these precious souls while I was away, as it was known that the clergy and town were very strongly against anything new or different! From the niece of these women I learned how they stood staunch and firm against the open and vicious attacks of the entire village. The young woman, after explaining how her aunts went through this man-made hell, declared herself and within a week we had fifteen believers in this village. All the two women had to say when I came to see them again was "Oh *Don* Jenabe, it is so hard to be a Bahá'í and love your neighbors when they are so nasty." Are these not living proof of the nearness of God as stated by Bahá'u'lláh, *I am nearer to thee than thy own life's vein?*

No matter how long or deeply we study the glorious teachings of Bahá'u'lláh, we will forever stand thunderstruck at the tremendous power that lies hidden within the revealed word. One day I had a very bright young man say, after I had explained the Faith to him, "Religion is life and very important. One must study for years. I like Bahá'í, and think it is beautiful. Perhaps after years of studying the teachings I will become a Bahá'í." I told him that was wonderful, because one of the principles of the Faith was individual investigation of the truth. He then asked if he might see the Bahá'í prayer book. As he read one of Bahá'u'lláh's prayers, his first reaction was wonderment and astonishment, followed by tears. When he finished, I looked at him and said, "What do you think?" He replied, "Man, I've studied enough. I know this is from God, and I'm ready to become a Bahá'í right now."

CHAPTER
16

THERE WAS A TIME when I went off into the Seri Indian Reservation with a Mayan believer. The Seris are very primitive and reported to be hostile but, since the reservation was a goal of the Nine Year Plan, the attempt had to be made. My Mayan companion and I met in Mexico City, visited and taught all the way north. As usual our sole provisions for our journey were faith and reliance upon God, and the very firm conviction that God always keeps His promise.

The last stop at the end of the road was Kino, with no contact with western civilization from here on. As we asked directions, in walked two Indians, both with long hair, very different from the Mexican-Indians we were used to. One had a red ribbon around his head, only one trouser leg and a piece of cloth for the other leg, a pair of dark glasses (well, almost: one lens was completely gone and the other was only a piece of jagged glass) and a smile that was a wonder to behold. One could feel the wildness of them, like a deer or fawn that is curious but ready to take flight on the instant. I asked one of them if he would care to guide us to Desenboque, the main Seri village, but he couldn't as he had come by boat; he did invite me, however, to visit him at his home in Santa Rosa. We could have used a guide because there is no road and the village lies about ninety kilometers back in the bush. But with hearts full of the love of God, and prayers streaming from our lips, we started out anyway with God as our guide. I just followed tire tracks through the sand, and every time we came to one going one way and some going the other, we said, "Yá Bahá'u'lláh-Abhá" – and took the wrong route. Talk about being guided – for twelve to fourteen hours we gave pamphlets in every *ranchero* between Kino and Punto Chueco. Not *once* did we follow the right track. Late in the evening we arrived at Santa Rosa but, to our surprise, there was no village, not even a house, only a desolate beach. Just then we heard our first jeep of the day, and rushed off to intercept it.

My first question to the driver was, "Where is Santa Rosa?"

He replied, "You just came out of Santa Rosa."

"But," I cried, "nobody lives there."

"Who said anybody lives there?"

"How far to Desenboque?" I changed the subject.

"Seventy-two kilometers," he replied.

"Oh dear!" I said. "I guess it's back to Kino because both of my gas tanks are almost empty."

"That's not necessary," he explained. "You just turn left up ahead and go to the beach – the place is called Punto Chueco. I buy fish from the Seris, and you tell my boy to sell you some gas for the Kino price."

Now I ask you – are all His servants or not, and do all abide by His bidding?

I thanked this man and thus stopped at Punto Chueco, and who should be waiting for us but my wild man of the morning! First, my Mayan friend, Celestino, began giving the message to several Seris who came around while I gassed up, then the wild man arrived, saying, "Come with me." So I followed him down the beach and ended up several miles away where there was another large group of Seris, whom I told about the coming of Bahá'u'lláh. We slept on the beach and at the first glimmer of dawn I was awakened by José (my new Seri friend) who was very busy examining my mattress. He said, "I am going with you to Desenboque." So, off we went, bouncing down the beach. Next, a very strange thing happened. I began to talk about Bahá'u'lláh, then Celestino would talk — and for seventy-two kilometers we talked and talked and talked, but the odd thing was that José never once asked a question or made a comment. His sole contribution was "turn here," "turn there," "go straight." Celestino and I covered everything in the Bahá'í writings, I am sure, from Shaykh-Ahmad-i-Ahsá'í to Shoghi Effendi, including the Divine Plan and the administration, yet our Seri never uttered a word of conversation.

Upon our arrival in Desenboque, the natives swarmed around the truck, began to rock it and apparently intended to tip it over. Our José disappeared, and Celestino and I jumped out as we assumed it would be easier to pick ourselves up than to right the truck. As we jumped out, the Indians all gathered around and the attitude was hostile. My first words were, "We have come to tell you about God." Once more, as if one turned off the water, the hostility completely vanished and a chorus went up, "Oh, please let us talk about

God." We ended with six invitations to return to teach them more about Bahá'u'lláh, and we gave out literature. With these invitations, we were in, as now we had friends and places to return to, and so the Seris were opened to the Faith of God.

As we returned to Kino, our hearts were happy, but as we had finally run down, we said nothing. José, his usual self, said only "turn here," "turn there," "straight ahead." As we neared Punto Chueco (his home) I thought, "My friend José must not be very bright." I only thought this, and said nothing aloud. José then spoke, saying, "That is right. I'm not the smartest Seri Indian. There are a lot of Indians more intelligent than I am, but let me tell you something. I know what no other Seri knows, and that is that what you said about Bahá'u'lláh is true, and I know He's really God's messenger. No other Seri knows that."

I stopped the truck, my heart in my throat, my soul in consternation. Could this apparently simple boy read my mind? What's more, here was our first Seri declaration . . . astonishment is added to astonishment. I asked him if he truly believed in Bahá'u'lláh as God's new Messenger and if he wanted to be a Bahá'í. He assured us with enthusiasm that he did.

"However," he said, "I have one very important question."

"Please ask all the questions you like."

"Well, I just love to drink. When I am drunk I'm happy. I would rather get drunk than anything else in this world. What do we Bahá'ís believe about drinking?"

He was holding the registration card in his hand at the time. I reached over, took the card, and replied,

"God loves you very, very much; more than any mother loves her children. He looks down upon us, His children, with this tender love that man cannot even understand, and He sees us getting drunk. He knew, even before science found out, that alcohol destroys the mind, the liver and general health — that it is bad for us. He also sees us wasting money that our wives and children need for food and clothing. He sees us get drunk and fight with our friends and neighbors, making enemies of those whom we should love. He sees this and as a tender, loving Father guiding His child, He says: 'Oh my son whom I love so very much, for your real health and happiness, please don't drink because it will destroy you.' "

José sat for some minutes in meditation, then, with a very warm smile, he said, "That's good, very good" — and reclaimed his card.

I asked Celestino to read a prayer, whereupon our new Bahá'í brother snatched the prayer book out of the Mayan's hands and proceeded to read most beautifully a prayer of Bahá'u'lláh's. This was my confirmation that I alone qualify as the ignorant savage, for once again I had learned many lessons from our so-called primitive brothers.

CHAPTER
17

THE YEAR 128 was the year in which the Universal House of Justice called for international traveling teachers, and I immediately responded. Elaine, that pure-hearted and selfless Knight of Bahá'u'lláh, was having difficulty with the language and customs of Mexico. Schooling for children was non-existent in the areas in which I was working. Since I would be off for days on end – sometimes even months – teaching in remote areas of Mexico, the family felt they could not cope alone in such an unfamiliar culture. The Universal House of Justice responded, stating they would suggest that I remain in Mexico.

Again I can only say, "I long with all my heart to sacrifice something for the Cause of God." No year in my life has ever been so fruitful in the hundreds of declarations or in the miles traveled. I lived in a little tent and went from village to village. Every night, home was wherever I happened to be. I taught all through Central America on my way to the Intercontinental Conference in Panama. Every day saw miracles such as I have already described. I will mention here only a few that were just a little out of the ordinary.

We were in a little village called La Fé (which translated means 'The Faith'), Oaxaca, running the movie *His Name Shall be One*, with a Spanish-language tape. This night I had two youths and a Mayan couple with me. After the movie, the first ever seen there, the boys put the equipment away and I noted something unusual: all the males, including children, carried machetes. One person, as spokesman, came forward and demanded that I show the movie again. I pointed out that the light plant needed gas that we did not have, and it would be impossible.

"You show the movie again or we are going to cut you all up with our machetes." The men all waved their machetes over their heads and cried, "Yea! Yea! Yea!"

The Mayan couple ran over and locked themselves in the truck.

I answered, "You will just have to start cutting," and sat there calmly.

The leader called a conference, returned and stated, "You show the movie again or we are going to cut up your truck and you will be unable to leave." The action was repeated in chorus by everyone with "Yea! Yea! Yea! "

My reply was the same.

So, back to the conference, and this time the spokesman returned and said in a very gentle voice, "If you will please show the movie again we will all become Bahá'ís." Once more all raised their machetes over their heads and shouted in unison, "Yea! Yea! Yea!"

I explained, "My friends and brothers, I can't show the movie as I do not have sufficient gasoline for the light plant, but even if I could, I wouldn't on those conditions. One's belief in Bahá'u'lláh springs from the heart and soul and is not conditioned upon seeing a movie. In the future, when any of you have this true belief in God's new Messenger, we will accept you with open arms into the Cause of God." With that, I folded up my table and chair and retired to my tent for the night. This was not the only time I have been threatened. One time I was even arrested and put in jail, and in this manner was able to proclaim the Message of Bahá'u'lláh to an entire town, otherwise an impossible feat.

On another occasion, in the town of Ixtepeji, Oaxaca, where in the past I had confronted trouble with the church and various people, after I showed the movie and told them about Bahá'u'lláh, the people sat as if in a trance for a long time. Later, when I was in my tent and nearly asleep, the church bells went wild and soon, sure enough, I could hear footsteps gathering around my tent. I thought, "Oh, oh! Here it comes." But was I surprised when they began to sing! They sang all the religious songs they knew, there in the high sierras, with a full mountain moon and all gathered around my tent — singing to me songs of God's love and love of God. My heart pleads with you, oh my friends, abandon your abodes of dust that you also might taste the delights of this paradise of confirmation while yet walking upon this earth!

In Yucatán we had marvelous victories — in one evening thirty-three declarations. The most we had anywhere else in one evening was nineteen in Oaxaca.

When I was nearly finished in the southeast of Mexico, I received a letter from the International Goals

Committee asking if I could stop in Africa on my way to Haifa for the election of the Universal House of Justice. I was going to Haifa as a member of the National Assembly of Mexico. I still had the northern part of Mexico to cover and was very busy. I also wanted to spend a little time with my family before going to Iran and Haifa, so I threw the letter in my suitcase, saying to myself it wasn't possible. That night after the movie, the motor fell out of my truck – the first trouble in thousands of miles. Coincidence? Perhaps, but read on. The following night, the last projector bulb I had burned out. Well? I borrowed a projector from the American Embassy in Yucatán and arranged for them to get us more bulbs. Several nights later, a film, tapes and equipment were stolen from my truck. As I lay in my tent that night, the movie was definitely over. I said, "All right, Bahá'u'lláh, I got the message. I'm going to Africa." When I arrived in Mexico City we received a phone call that most of the equipment had been recovered.

CHAPTER

18

ON MY FIRST NIGHT in West Africa there were two declarations in an area that had had none for some time. I can summarize Africa with two accounts, which speak for my whole trip.

In Togo, as we rode on a motor scooter, kilometer after kilometer in the blazing sun, I asked my host if we could perhaps stop at the next village and sit in the shade for a half hour since we were early. We did so and, of course, as we pulled up in the shade, some children and a few adults gathered around. No one spoke English, no one spoke Spanish, no one spoke French; they just spoke *Ave*. I began to sing that little song about clapping your hands, stamping your feet, and saying Alláh'u'Abhá. Soon the entire village was under the tree singing, and I will never forget the picture as we left after our half hour of rest – every man, woman and child standing with their faces filled with happiness and light singing that African melody of Alláh'u'Abhá and waving goodbye. Yes, for me, that tells you about Africa.

One other incident that took place in Africa I would like to share with you. I met a pioneer couple in

Nigeria. They were practically children, but oh, what children! These are the real children of the Crimson Ark, the Kingdom of Abhá. The man had finally received his degree in education and they wrote to the appropriate committee, saying that they would pioneer anywhere in the world he could get work. This committee replied, explaining that it would be better if a little experience was secured first. They got jobs, apartment, and so on, then with all details settled, their names came up for pilgrimage, and off they went to the land of their heart's desire. There they met the members of the Universal House of Justice, and told them of their pioneering plans. After consultation with this body, these stalwart warriors of Bahá'u'lláh went to the airline, traded in their return tickets to the United States and bought one-way tickets to Lagos, Nigeria. Surely here are the most beautiful examples of courage, dedication and *I lay all my affairs in Thy hand*. On the airplane, frightened, not knowing anyone — they were praying, when a stranger walked up.

"Where are you going?" he asks.

"Lagos, Nigeria," is the reply.

"What are you going to do there?"

"Look for work."

"What kind of work do you do?"

"I'm a schoolteacher," said the man.

"Thank God," the stranger exclaimed. "I work for the largest American School in Nigeria and we are desperate for teachers."

Thus armed with jobs, apartment and car, they were anxious to get on with their only real work, namely service to the Cause of God. They contacted the local Bahá'ís in Lagos and every night prayed together for guidance to reach the hearts of the people. Then came a letter, I don't know where from, advising them that I was coming and would show them how to teach in mass conversion areas. You can well imagine the excitement attending my arrival. It was agreed that what we needed to start with was a place not too near the city, plus a good interpreter.

We can read and we can talk about the pure-hearted African Bahá'ís but until it is seen and experienced, one has no idea of the reality. Everyone with faces as radiant as the sun and those eyes, the windows of the soul, sparkling like stars. My heart swells and throbs with such a deep, tender love for them by just remembering. Peter, one of many such true believers and soldiers in God's Cause, said, "Let us go to my village. It is out of town and I can interpret."

"How far away is your village?" I asked.

"About 300 miles," he replied.

Thus it was settled, and with the car filled with prayer, song and meditation, we sallied forth to learn about mass conversion. As we prayed, our hearts throbbed with love for one another, and as we sang with all the enthusiasm of our hearts the praises and glorifications to God, the car no longer even touched the road, as mile after mile sped by. At lunchtime, we stopped in the shade of a small village, and I set out to give the beautiful message of Bahá'u'lláh to the people who gathered. Some schoolteachers invited us back to tell them more about this new and beautiful message from God. I explained to my companions that we need go no further, as here we already had opened a village. When people invite you to return so they can study, and give their names and addresses, that town is surely open to the Cause of God.

Many times the ones that at first show interest do not accept, but always God guides us to those hearts He wants. However, once again my African brothers, with love, joy and laughter, would listen to none of my suggestions to turn back. They loaded me again into the car and off we floated to our destination.

Upon our arrival, everyone but Peter and I went off to the center of the village. We stopped at the chief's house (a relative of Peter's) to pay our respects, get permission to hold a meeting and arrange to spend the night. The chief was delighted, and being a very intelligent and highly educated man, he even offered to help with the interpreting. As we left his house, I said, "Come on Peter, let's go this way."

Peter, with eyes dancing, replied, "But Caldwell, that is the long way to the center of town; I know, I grew up here."

"Come on, Peter, let's go this way anyhow," I insisted.

Finally, as one would concede a whim to a child, Peter, with his great good nature, started off with me in the wrong direction. As we walked on, we met three most beautiful women, so tall, so straight, so elegant, walking away from the center of the village.

"Oh, Peter, Peter!" I cried, "Please invite them to the meeting." We stopped and Peter asked them. They turned right around and went with us to the meeting place.

Before the meeting, I prayed with all the fervor of my heart and soul, "Please, God, this couple has given so much and these, my soul brothers of Africa, are so on fire with Thy Cause; show them the way to win Thy victories."

First, I gave the message as truly, clearly, and simply as I could, then I opened the meeting for questions. How wide awake and alert was my audience! With my heart throbbing with the love of God and love for these, His children, after every question I would say to myself the Greatest Name, and then answer. Praise be to God that I had obeyed my Guardian and studied the Qur'án, for many here were Muslims. It seemed with each question I instinctively knew whether it was Muslim, Christian or Ju-Ju who asked it. At first, the chief translated, then later Peter. For five hours the questions came. At the end, one man stood up and said, "With that question you just answered, for the first time in my life my heart has been satisfied regarding God and religion and I wish to belong to this Faith."

That night we had nine declarations. Then, for three more hours, at the home of the chief, I talked to him alone. As nearly I can remember, his words were, "I would be turning my back on my Lord Christ if I did not accept Bahá'u'lláh." This made number ten.

We were just up and about in the morning when one of those most beautiful women we met on the road the evening before came to the door. She declared, "I stayed up all night and prayed and I know this is true. I accept with all my heart and so do my entire family." Of course, we explained that her family must come and declare for themselves. She assured us that on our next visit, this they would do.

Well, if we floated in, we had no words to describe how we got out. *What tongue can voice my thanks to Thee.* These were only two instances and we could recount a hundred – all different, all beautiful, wholly spiritual –

121

which took place in that illuminated continent of Africa.

I went on to Iran, then Haifa for the election of the Universal House of Justice, then back to Mexico where I was privileged to help construct the Amelia Collins Institute in San Francisco Acatepec, in Puebla state. I was director of this school. Every day was an experience, every student a jewel of great price, only needing to be polished in the deepening water of Bahá'u'lláh's ocean.

EPILOGUE

THIS NARRATIVE STARTED as a report requested by the Universal House of Justice. They asked
us to send in the stories of the Knights of Bahá'u'lláh in
BE 120. I dutifully sent in my report and then received a
note of thanks requesting that I get it published. The
first part of the book covered my life up to BE 126
(1970–1), while as I write this Epilogue it is now BE 146
(1991). As you finish the first section, you can feel that
Jenabe thought he had it made spiritually. In fact as I
traveled and taught with Hand of the Cause Dr.
Muhájir, every day he would ask me to pray for him
that he might die a firm Bahá'í. I honestly never understood this. This most wonderful man not only loved
Bahá'u'lláh, but gave his every breath and minute to
Him in the most dedicated service, yet he was con-
cerned about his spiritual well-being! It is true that I
had read many times what Bahá'u'lláh said about no
man knowing his own end and how even the most
devout Bahá'í can, at the very last moment of life, fall
into the nethermost fire. Reading it and understanding
it are two different things. I did mass teaching in fifty-

four countries and fully realize that it was not Jenabe who did it. Whose teachings are they? Whose holy spirit is it? Whose divine concourse on high is it? Who sends the waiting souls to us? Who sends us to them? Who inspires our hearts with His divine inspiration? Of course every Bahá'í will instantly say, "Bahá'u'lláh". We have a very explicit warning in this regard from 'Abdu'l-Bahá:

> The more one is severed from the world, from desires, from human affairs and conditions, the more impervious does one become to the tests of God. Tests are a means by which a soul is measured as to its fitness, and proven out by its own acts. God knows its fitness beforehand, and also its unpreparedness, but man with an ego, would not believe himself unfit unless proof were given him. Consequently his susceptibility to evil is proven to him when he falls into the tests, and the tests are continued until the soul realizes its own unfitness, then remorse and regret tend to root out the weakness. The same test comes again in greater degree, until it is shown that a former weakness has become a strength, and the power to overcome evil has been established.
>
> (Tablets of 'Abdu'l-Bahá Vol. 5, p. 234)

Now I know and realize what it means and, like Dr. Muhájir, I pray ardently every day that I might die a firm Bahá'í. In BE 133 (1978), my marriage of thirty-one years fell apart. That most wonderful and dedicated Knight of Bahá'u'lláh, Elaine Caldwell, whom I had taken for granted for all those years, gave up. Elaine is truly one of the unsung heroes in the Cause of God.

This woman is totally selfless, never complains, stays away from conflict and contention, and lives a truly Bahá'í life. If anyone has the title of 'Saint', it should be Elaine Caldwell, a true Knight of Bahá'u'lláh.

Up to this time, I had no patience with any of the Bahá'ís who on every side were giving up on their marriages. "How is this possible?" I would rant and rave in my holier-than-thou attitude. Now I know, and I understand the hell and anguish of it and my heart overflows with love and tenderness for these souls. There is no way I could ever have understood this hell if I had not gone through it myself. Only God knows how I have suffered and what I have lost due entirely to my own negligence.

So dear reader, I was plunged back into the pit of blackness and into the desolation of night. Though my sins be as many as the individual grains of sand upon the beach, God's forgiveness, grace and mercy are as the drops in the mighty ocean. When the waves of this sea wash over the sand upon the beach it is able to clean the sand of all contamination. Only one thing has been light upon light during this period and that is serving the Cause of Bahá'u'lláh however and wherever He has seen fit.

My prayer to God that I said when I was in the depths of despair, has been answered. This is that prayer:

> *My God, my Beloved, my Heart's Desire. From the very depths of my soul and the fullness of my heart, I rededicate myself to Thee and beg Thy forgiveness and pardon for all of my past and future sins and transgressions and plead with every fiber of my inner and*

*outer being for your protection and that I may be pro-
tected by Thee from myself. I pray that I may submit
myself to Thy will with absolute obedience, follow in
Thy footsteps and dedicate my very heart, my soul,
my life, my breath, my heartbeat, my movement and
my stillness to Thy service and Thy Cause. I vow not
to become entangled in the affairs of the world or side-
tracked from Thy service and Thy Cause. O my most
Beloved of my heart and soul, please, I beg of Thee
with a humble and lacerated heart, to assist me with
Thy Holy Spirit, surround me with Thy love, guide
my footsteps in this dark world. Let me be a candle of
light for others, an ocean of love for Thy creatures, a
unifier of peoples and nations and a token of Thy
infinite love, grace and spirit to every soul you put me
into contact with.*

My heart and my soul pulsate with such a nearness to
God that only those seated at that same heavenly feast
are aware of it. *And the Lord alone shall be exalted in that
Day.* Although I walk upon this earth, I am not part of
it. My soul wanders in a realm where on every side
only the Glory of God can be heard, and although I
say "from night to Knight" both night and day have no
meaning in this timeless, sanctified reality.

The sky is more blue, the sun warmer, the flowers
more fragrant and the colors of the rainbow more brilliant, and I have come out into a new creation. A
creation where heart and soul rule supreme, and body
and mind are harmonized in servitude to the Cause of
God and the world of humanity. The world knows no
happiness like this happiness, for it is complete. How
longingly mankind wants and seeks this reality of joy,

then chooses the false gods of materialism, only to find emptiness, or, at the most, a temporary enjoyment that is gone like the blink of an eye. I cry out, with all the love God has deposited in my heart for all of you, from the heaven of wonder and delight – come with me, sorrowful ones, lonely ones, loved ones, to the ocean of God's love and immerse yourselves in permanent and everlasting joy.

From night to Knight, from darkness blacker than space into the most glorious light. With a heart galvanized to action, on my steed of steadfastness in His Cause, and with total dedication, I sally forth.

My beloved Guardian, Shoghi Effendi, had inscribed our names as Knights of Bahá'u'lláh, to be deposited at the Shrine of Bahá'u'lláh. On the map he had with him in London at the time he took his flight to the Abhá Kingdom, the beloved Guardian had in his own hand called our goal of the Aleutians an outstanding achievement of the Ten Year Crusade. My heart is crushed and rivers of tears flow at the insignificance of our accomplishments. I vow with all my heart, soul, and power, to redeem, if possible and God willing, this high honor showered upon us.

Then shall the knights of the Lord, assisted by His grace from on high, strengthened by faith, aided by the power of understanding, and reinforced by the legions of the Covenant, arise and make manifest the truth of the verse, "Behold the confusion that hath befallen the tribes of the defeated." (World Order of Bahá'u'lláh, p. 17.)

FINIS